FORBIDDEN TERRITORY

"You must think me bold and shameless, coming here like this," Rupa said, as she wound her arms around Cimarron's naked body.

"I think you're a lovely lady and I'm glad you came to keep me company," Cimarron said. His right hand roved over her flannel nightdress and then under it.

Cimarron eased Rupa down on her back and then lay down beside her. She sat up.

"Gypsy women aren't supposed to do this," she said, as she slipped her nightdress over her head, cast it aside, lay down very close and embraced him.

Cimarron was speechless. For someone in forbidden territory, she sure knew her way around. . . .

D1559731

SIGNET Westerns You'll Enjoy by Leo P. Kelley

(0451)

*Prices slightly higher in Canada

16
CIMARRON
AND THE SCALP HUNTERS

BY

LEO P. KELLEY

A SIGNET BOOK

NEW AMERICAN LIBRARY

PUBLISHER'S NOTE

This novel is a work of fiction. Names, characters, places, and incidents either are the product of the author's imagination or are used fictitiously, and any resemblance to actual persons, living or dead, or events, is entirely coincidental.

NAL BOOKS ARE AVAILABLE AT QUANTITY DISCOUNTS WHEN USED TO PROMOTE PRODUCTS OR SERVICES. FOR INFORMATION PLEASE WRITE TO PREMIUM MARKETING DIVISION, NEW AMERICAN LIBRARY, 1633 BROADWAY, NEW YORK, NEW YORK 10019.

Copyright © 1985 by Leo P. Kelley

The first chapter of this book previously appeared in Cimarron and the Prophet's People, the fifteenth volume in this series.

SIGNET TRADEMARK REG. U.S. PAT. OFF. AND FOREIGN COUNTRIES
REGISTERED TRADEMARK—MARCA REGISTRADA
HECHO EN CHICAGO, U.S.A.

SIGNET, SIGNET CLASSIC, MENTOR, PLUME, MERIDIAN and NAL BOOKS are published by New American Library, 1633 Broadway, New York, New York 10019

First Printing, July, 1985

1 2 3 4 5 6 7 8 9

PRINTED IN THE UNITED STATES OF AMERICA

CIMARRON . . .

. . . he was a man with a past he wanted to forget and a future uncertain at best and dangerous at worst. Men feared and secretly admired him. Women desired him. He roamed the Indian Territory with a Winchester '73 in his saddle scabbard, an Army Colt in his hip holster, and a bronc he had broken beneath him. He packed his guns loose, rode his horse hard, and no one dared throw gravel in his boots. Once he had an ordinary name like other men. But a tragic killing forced him to abandon it and he became known only as Cimarron. *Cimarron*, in Spanish, meant wild and unruly. It suited him. *Cimarron*.

1

Cimarron awoke in a room filled with early-morning sunlight, and for a confused moment he didn't know where he was.

But then, as he became aware of the warm body of the woman lying in the bed beside him, the woman whose tousled black hair framed her lovely face and whose voluptuous body exuded a faint musky odor, he remembered.

He had come to visit her soon after arriving the night before in Muskogee in Creek Nation. He had left his prisoners at the town's jail in charge of the Creek Lighthorseman who was on duty there and then he had come directly here to Serena Farthing's house. She had been, he recalled with pleasure, delighted to see him again, and he had told her that she looked just as lovely as ever. It wasn't long—first they had had coffee and some gingerbread Serena had baked—before they were upstairs, undressed, and in bed together.

He sighed softly, a sound of complete contentment, as he recalled how he had coupled—more than once during the lusty night—with Serena, who was now lying so still beside him, her knees drawn up, her arms flung out, a faint smile on her face as she slept soundly. She had been a hot fire and he had been the kindling she had so eagerly consumed.

He drew a deep breath and then stretched to rid his saddle-sore body of its stiffness. He turned over on his side and whispered her name.

She didn't stir.

"Wake up, Serena. I got to be going." He bent over and kissed her cheek.

She moaned faintly, reached out, and drew him closer to her. He dropped back down on the bed again and wrapped his arms around her. He nuzzled her neck as her hand fluttered teasingly first over his sun-bronzed and scarred face and then down along his lean and tautly muscled body.

"Don't go."

"Got to."

She opened her eyes, shook her head, and drew him even closer to her so that he could feel the heat of her body against his own and her faintly moist breath on his chest.

"But we'll get together again like this," he promised her. "You can count on it."

"Stay just a little while longer."

"Would like to. Can't. Got some prisoners waiting on me. Three real hardcases. Two men, Lewis Detweiler and Zeke Bantry, and one woman, Jane Perkins—the three of them ran a real bad operation up in the Three Forks Area that was supposed to be religious but was really an unholy business involving everything from sex for sale to murder. Detweiler called himself the Prophet, and him along with Bantry and Perkins made life hell for the people they enticed into joining up with them.

"Plus I also got me a whiskey-peddling puppeteer to pick up name of Doctor Lucius Dexter. Every last one of the four's going to take up lodgings back in Judge Parker's hotel in Fort Smith."

Serena raised her head and looked into Cimarron's eyes. "I wish we could stay like this forever," she murmured as she ran her fingers through the thick tangle of black hair that covered his chest. "Just the two of us."

"And let the rest of the world go to hell in a handbasket?"

"Mmmm-hmmmm."

"That's a prospect I don't altogether deplore. But it's not exactly one you could call practical, I reckon you're willing to admit."

"I can't be practical when I'm with you like this, Cimarron. Surely you must know that by now. I can be romantic. I can be sensual. I can be lusty. Even as bawdy as I was last night. But practical? Oh, my, no!"

He kissed her again, slid out from between the sheets, and began to dress.

As he did so, Serena sat back against her pillow, which she had propped up against the bed's brass headboard, her breasts bare, the top sheet covering only the lower half of her body. "When will I see you again?"

"Can't say for certain. Like I said before, I got to get my four prisoners to the jail in Fort Smith and then see what Marshal Upham might have lined up for me."

He buttoned his faded jeans and then sat down on the edge of the bed and pulled on his dusty black army boots, noting as he did so that both heels were badly worn down. "Serena, I've been meaning to ask you something." He buttoned his flannel shirt and then tied his blue bandanna around his neck. "Those two jaspers who engineered that crooked race I won on your horse, Fleet of Foot, some days ago—did the possemen who went chasing after that pair ever catch up with them?"

Serena shook her head. "They found neither Simkins nor his rider, Prendergast."

"Then that means I'm out the twenty dollars I bet on myself to win that race since those two ran off with all the money that was bet on it, along with the five-hundred-dollar stake that was supposed to be split between your winning horse and the one Prendergast was aboard."

Serena held up her arms as an invitation, and Cimarron, after buckling his cartridge belt around his hips, sat down on the bed beside her. She gave him an affectionate hug and then declared, "Prendergast and Simkins weren't the only ones to steal money from me recently."

"Somebody else did too?"

9

"Yes. A gypsy woman named Mala."

"What happened?"

"Well, some gypsies came to town after you left following the stakes race, and the woman they all called Mala started telling fortunes out at their camp on the edge of town. When I heard that, I went out there right away to see her."

"She told your fortune, did she, this lady named Mala?"

Serena blushed and looked away.

"What'd she say?"

"She told me I was unlucky in love." Serena looked back at Cimarron. "She read my hand, Cimarron, and it was as if she could see into the very darkest part of my heart. I never told a soul about how I've never been able to hold on to you, but Mala saw it in my hand almost immediately. She said she saw a handsome but trifling man in my life and she told me how sorry she was for me because I'd let myself get mixed up with a silver-tongued seducer. That's what she called you, Cimarron. A 'silver-tongued seducer.'"

"Honey, I'm not trifling with you. Nor am I nothing more than a silver-tongued seducer. Why, I take being with you real serious every single time."

"Maybe you do, Cimarron. But then you always go away and I never know when—or even if—I'll ever see you again! That's no way for a woman to have to live, a woman like me, who has so much love stored up inside her and who only wants a husband who—"

Cimarron shifted position on the bed, becoming decidedly uneasy as Serena rambled on about her dreams and desires, all of which seemed to be centered on him.

"—and Mala divined, she told me, that I was unlucky in love because someone had put a curse on my money," Serena continued.

"A curse on your money?"

"She said she could remove the curse for me and then, once it was gone, I—you and I—we—" Serena began to weep, her face hidden in her hands. Then, recovering,

10

she sniffed and said, "I was to take all my savings out of the bank and bring the money to Mala."

"Every cent of your savings?"

"Yes. She said if I didn't bring it all, the curse would only stay on that part of the money I kept and you would—I wouldn't— So I brought her every penny I had in the world—eighty-seven dollars. Mala took the money and she put it in a handkerchief, which she sewed up. Then we prayed together. Mala shouted. She wept. She rolled about on the floor in a kind of frenzy. Then she gave me back the handkerchief containing my money and she swore to me that she had removed the curse from it.

"But, she said, I mustn't open the handkerchief for three days. If I didn't wait the full three days, she said, the money would turn into worthless paper. I went home and I did just what she told me to do. I put the handkerchief away in a drawer and not until three days had passed did I rip out the stitches and open the handkerchief." Serena began again to weep, more loudly this time.

Cimarron reached out and silently caressed her bare shoulder.

"The money wasn't in the handkerchief," she wailed. "There was nothing in the handkerchief but strips of worthless old newspapers. Cimarron, I couldn't believe my eyes. I was distraught. I thought I had made some sort of mistake. I checked the calendar, but I hadn't made a mistake. I had waited the three days like I was supposed to do. So I hurried off to the gypsy camp to tell Mala that something had gone wrong. But, when I got there, the gypsies were all gone."

"You sure were taken for a sleigh ride, honey," Cimarron told Serena.

"I know that now!"

"My guess is that when Mala was rolling around on the floor and otherwise getting into the spirit of your prayer session, she was also busy switching handkerchiefs. She sewed your money up in one, but she had another just like it hidden away someplace with torn newspapers already sewed up inside it."

11

"That woman! If I ever see her again, I'll kill her," Serena wailed, soundlessly pounding her fists on the bed. "I thought—hoped—that at last I'd finally found a way to hold on to you. But I hadn't. It looks to me like I'll keep on losing you just as I recently lost my eighty-seven dollars to that scheming gypsy Mala."

"Honey," Cimarron said softly as he used his thumbs to wipe the tears from Serena's cheeks, "you don't really lose me like it seems you think you do. It's just that I'm a fiddle-footed sort of man who's always got to be on the move so he can find out what's up the crick and on the other side of the mountain. I just can't seem to light in one place for long. I'll probably spend the rest of my life looking at the world from between a horse's ears. But I always come on back to you, don't I?"

"Yes." Serena sniffed.

"And we have good times together every time I do, don't we?"

"Yes." Another sniff.

"Well, then, there you go, honey!"

Serena stared at him, a puzzled expression on her face.

He took both of her hands in his. "If you'd really went and lost me, it's for sure and certain that you'd never see me again. But I keep coming to call on you and we two keep popping into bed together, so you've not lost me, don't you see that?"

"When you talk like that, I do. But then, after you've left me all alone again to fret myself to a frazzle, I feel like I never really had you in the first place despite the fact that we— Well, you know what I mean."

"Liking somebody a lot don't mean you've got to put them in a box with a lock on it, honey."

"Oh, Cimarron, do get out of here if you're so hell-bent on going. You muddle my mind."

He leaned forward and lightly kissed the tip of her pert nose. "Be seeing you, honey."

"Soon, I hope," she said somewhat wistfully as he rose, slipped into his buckskin jacket, and clapped his black slouch hat on his head.

12

"Me too," he told her, and then, after touching the brim of his hat to her, he left the bedroom and made his way down the stairs and out of the house.

Late that same afternoon, the train Cimarron was aboard with his four prisoners, whom he had picked up at the jail in Muskogee after leaving Serena, pulled into the Missouri, Kansas, and Texas railroad's depot at Gibson Station in Creek Nation.

"I'm hungry," Jane Perkins announced, and when Cimarron did not respond, she added, "There's a vendor outside selling sandwiches and milk." When he still did not respond, she muttered, "You know what you are, starpacker? What you are is the meanest son of a bitch that ever came down the pike, *that's* what you are!"

Still he said nothing as he continued staring through the open window at the crowd milling about the depot. The sudden sound of a brass band beginning to play caught his attention and he watched the band members in their red uniforms replete with gold braid march past the depot. Leading them were two men carrying a sign stretched between them which read:

THIS WAY TO THE ANNUAL COWETA DISTRICT FAIR

A faint memory stirred in his mind as the whiskey peddler, who was one of his four prisoners, whined, "These handcuffs are cutting into my wrists."

"Shut up, Doc," Zeke Bantry barked, and gave Dr. Lucius Dexter a sharp nudge in the ribs.

What is it, Cimarron asked himself, about the Coweta District Fair that's nagging at my mind? It's just another fair full of prize pumpkins, fat heifers, and country bumpkins and their ladies . . .

Ladies! That's it, he thought. Delilah, he thought. Just before I left her in Muskogee after I won that horse race, she told me she might not be there when I got back. Said she'd accepted an invitation to come on up here to see the fair. Well, now, I wonder, did she?

Cimarron scanned the faces of the people milling around the depot, but he saw no sign of Delilah. It's a real long

13

shot, he thought, an outside chance. But one, he suddenly decided, I'll take. Why the hell not? I've got nothing to lose and maybe Delilah to gain. Now that I've dillied with Serena back in Muskogee, maybe here in Gibson Station I might just get lucky and have me a chance to dally with Delilah.

"Let's go," he snapped, and got to his feet. When Detweiler, grumbling, also rose, so did the others, all of whom were handcuffed together, the right wrist of one prisoner to the left wrist of another prisoner.

He followed them down the aisle, and once outside on the platform, he displayed his badge and the train's conductor obligingly delayed the train's departure, giving Cimarron time to remove his bay from a slatted cattle car near the caboose.

He climbed into the saddle and barked, "March!"

His prisoners marched.

Less than twenty minutes later, all four of them had been safely lodged in the Gibson Station jail, and Cimarron, pocketing the receipts for them that he had been given by the Creek Lighthorseman who was in charge of the jail, left his bay at the livery stable and then made his way to where the Coweta District Fair was in loud and exuberant progress in a meadow not far from the Katy's depot.

Keeping his eyes peeled for a glimpse of Delilah, he made his way out past tents where cakes were being displayed by their makers, women who hoped to win a prize for their culinary art; past freshly picked produce piled high on tables; past a man timing a milking contest in which the contestants were all seated on low three-legged stools as they bent to their task and the *tinging* of milk as it spurted into tin pails was the only sound to be heard.

He stopped for a moment to watch children riding a merry-go-round. Watching them and listening to the raucous music of the merry-go-round's calliope, Cimarron found himself remembering the time a traveling medicine show had come to the central Texas town near the

14

homeplace where he had grown up. He remembered now that wonderful day when he was nine years old and, emboldened by imagination, had become a soldier. As he rode his merry-go-round mount with General George Armstrong Custer riding at his side. Then, because he had shot straight and he had shot true, war-whooping Indians had died and General Custer had pinned a medal on his proud chest and the merry-go-round's calliope had played an arousing anthem to celebrate his heroism.

He was about to turn away, to leave his fond memories of that long-ago day behind him, when he happened to catch sight of a small boy standing not far away. He had his hands thrust deep in his pockets as he stared intently at the merry-go-round's brightly painted horses and other animals and at all the children so happily astride them.

Cimarron smiled, trapped again in a net of pleasant memories, and saw himself reflected in the nearby boy—in his patched pants, badly scuffed shoes, rapt expression, and awed eyes. He looked back at the merry-go-round, saw it once again with nine-year-old eyes, and found himself marveling as the rainbowed horses, the white-winged swans, and the single gilded lion, its mouth wide open in a roar that only children could hear, glided by him.

He went over to stand beside the boy. "You fixing to take yourself a ride on that thing once it stops?"

"Nope."

"How come you're not?"

A brief hesitation, a shy glance up at Cimarron, and then, stalwartly, "I only had but ten cents to spend and I already spent it over at the freak show so's I could get to see the two-headed calf they had in there in a big bottle filled full of alcohol. But it don't matter. That there ride"—the boy pointed a scornful finger at the merry-go-round—"it's for little kids."

"What's your name, boy?"

"Jamie. Jamie Watkins. What's yours?"

"Cimarron. Now maybe you've got a point about that ride being for little kids. Then again maybe you've not got such a good point. What I'm getting at is, I have a sort of hankering to ride that merry-go-round myself."

When Cimarron said no more, Jamie gave him another shy glance before asking, "Why don't you, then?"

"Well, I guess it's on account of I'm used to riding with a partner," he lied. "I'd feel sort of lost, not to mention real lonely, were I to try riding one of those horses without nobody siding me."

Cimarron wasn't looking directly at Jamie but he knew that the boy was looking up at him, and out of the corner of his eye he saw hope flare in the boy's eyes. "I was wondering," he quickly continued, "if I were to pay your way, to sort of make it up to you for you having to waste your time, would you be willing to take a ride with me?"

"Sure I will—if you really want me to."

"I want you to. So let's go, partner!"

They stepped up to the ticket seller's table and Cimarron bought two tickets, one of which he handed to Jamie, who stood fidgeting at his side. When the merry-go-round finally stopped, they boarded it together. Cimarron was about to help Jamie up onto the horse the boy had chosen—a mount on the outer row of animals that seemed to Cimarron to be as dazzling in its coat of red, white, and purple paint and golden glass eyes as any Christmas tree he had ever seen—but Jamie pulled away from him.

"I don't need no boost." He climbed quickly into the saddle, and moments later, as the calliope began to boom and bellow, the merry-go-round began to move once more in its circular path.

"*Whooppee!*" Jamie crowed, and lashed his slowly rising and falling mount with his leather reins while Cimarron, his boots tucked into his horse's stirrups, rode along beside his young companion, his hands on the metal pole that rose from his mount's body and his eyes on the container of rings that jutted out from a tall iron dispenser at the top of a stanchion that stood just beyond the arc of the merry-go-round.

"If you can catch the brass ring," Cimarron told Jamie, having to lean toward the boy and shout because of the squeals and screams of the children who were riding ahead of and behind him, "you get yourself a free ride."

"I can't reach that high," Jamie shouted back. "But you could, Cimarron. You're *big!* Let's switch horses!"

They did, and then, when both riders were horsed again, Cimarron, riding now on the outer circumference of the merry-go-round's platform, made a grab for the dispenser and got a plain iron ring. On the next revolution, he got another iron ring.

But on his third try he hooked the sought-after brass ring with his index finger and the whoop that he let out was even louder than Jamie's.

"You did it, Cimarron," the boy yelled. "You get a free ride!"

It was at that moment that Cimarron caught a blurred glimpse of Delilah strolling through the crowd on the arm of a dapper and mustachioed young man. He looked back over his shoulder, but she had vanished. As he came around again, he still could not see her. "Take these, Jamie," he said, and gave the boy beside him the three rings he had acquired. "You take the free ride that brass ring entitles you to if you want it. I'm far too saddle-sore for another trip on this stallion I've got under me."

"Thanks!" Jamie yelled as Cimarron dismounted and then leapt to the ground from the circling merry-go-round. He waited a moment for the vanished Jamie to reappear, and when the boy did, he waved farewell. Jamie waved happily back and shouted, just before he vanished again, "Thanks a lot, Cimarron!"

Cimarron hurried away from the merry-go-round and went in search of Delilah, leaving behind him the memory of the boy he was no longer who once had been, as Jamie Watkins was now, head over heels in love with the gaudy miracle of a merry-go-round.

Delilah, he discovered, wasn't at the milking contest. She wasn't in the tent where judges were now sampling the cakes that had been presented for prizes. Nor was she in the chattering crowd that was leaving the freak-show tent. He halted and looked around beginning to wonder if he had only imagined having seen her. But no, he told himself, he had definitely seen Delilah. He was sure of it. He considered shouting her name. But he didn't because he suddenly spotted her, the same mustachioed young man at her side, in front of a booth that sold novelties. He hurried over to it, and when he came up behind Delilah, he put his arms around her waist and squeezed.

"Ohhhh!" she cried. "Let me go!"

He squeezed harder and planted a kiss on the nape of her neck.

"I say, sir," declared the obviously startled young man with Delilah, "unhand the lady at once!"

Cimarron, ignoring the man, spun Delilah around to face him and kissed her on the lips. She squirmed and struggled to free herself from him, pummeling him with her fists, one of which held a blue-green peacock feather like the others for sale at the novelty booth.

He let her go and gave her a grin. "Honey, I sure am glad I remembered you were coming up here to the fair. I dropped by special just to try to round you up."

Delilah pursed her lips and gave him a suspicious look. "You probably came here to see the Egyptian dancing girls, not me."

"Egyptian dancing girls?" he repeated. "They got some of them here all the way from Egypt to dance for folks, have they? I didn't know that. But now that I do, maybe I'd better go and make their acquaintance. I've never yet met a genuine Egyptian dancing girl, but I've heard tell that they can do things with their bellies that would scandalize even the most sinful of men."

"Don't you dare," Delilah said, and seized his arm in an effort to restrain him.

"Delilah, do let go of that oaf," her young man demanded, a sour expression on his face.

Delilah's hand remained firmly on Cimarron's forearm. To her escort, she said, "You mustn't think naughty thoughts about me, Edwin. This gentleman is merely a dear friend of mine whom I haven't had the pleasure of seeing in, oh, ever so long." She gave Edwin a syrupy smile. "Would you excuse us for a moment, Edwin? There is some family business I must discuss with this gentleman. *Pressing* family business."

Without waiting for Edwin's approval or reply, Delilah quickly led Cimarron away from the man. When they were far enough away so that they could not be overheard by him, she asked, "Did you really come here in the hope of seeing me?"

"That's the gospel truth, honey. I remembered that the last time we met at the stakes race down in Muskogee you told me that you'd been invited to come up here to the fair."

"You're quite certain you didn't come here to see those foreign belly dancers in their veils and shamelessness?"

"It wasn't even to see the two-headed calf I hear tell they've got on display over in the freak show." He patted her cheek. "Let's us go someplace where we can cozy up to each other in private."

"But what about Edwin?"

"I'll be right back." Cimarron strode over to where Edwin was standing, his forlorn eyes on Delilah. When he returned to her side a few moments later, he took her arm and hurried her through the throng.

"Where are we going?" she asked him, and then, glancing back over her shoulder, "Where is *Edwin* going?"

"I told him you were hungry and wanted him to buy you a roast-beef sandwich and a slice of watermelon."

"You just told him I was hungry to get rid of him," Delilah accused.

"Sure, I did," Cimarron cheerfully admitted as they passed the depot and headed down Gibson Station's main street.

"Where are we going?" Delilah asked a second time.

She got her answer when Cimarron steered her into the lobby of the first hotel he came to and registered them both as Mr. and Mrs. John Smith. He took the key the smirking desk clerk handed him and guided Delilah up the stairs, down the hall, and finally into the room that bore a number matching the one penciled on the tag attached to the key in his hand.

He had no sooner closed the door behind him than Delilah was in his arms, whispering excitedly about how much she had missed him and how long it had been since the two of them had been together, and he was running his hands up and down her spine while simultaneously pressing his pelvis against hers.

They parted and both of them began to undress, Cimarron fumbling with buttons because of his growing excitement and Delilah demure as she dropped her peacock feather on a bedside table, unbuttoned and pulled her dress over her head, and let it fall on the floor by her feet.

Moments later, she lay nude on the bed, her sparkling eyes on Cimarron as he pulled off his boots and then his jeans. She giggled and pointed to his towering shaft. "Look at the great big soldier standing at attention!"

Cimarron lay down beside her and began to caress her, his hands roaming gently over the inviting hills and valleys of her voluptuous body.

She responded to his touch by eagerly returning his caresses with both her fingers and her lips, and as a result, he quickly reached a peak of arousal. He covered her, and then, because she was so wet and so willing, he easily and eagerly entered her. As he did so, he felt her arms encircle him and her legs wrap themselves around him. Cimarron was happy to be a prisoner bound to her and he began to move. Slowly at first. Then more quickly, until soon he was driving in and out of her and she, crying out wordlessly and clawing his back, soon reached what proved to be only the first in a swift series of shuddering climaxes.

Her loins continued to slap against Cimarron's until it seemed to him that his heart was about to burst within him. Ecstasy flowed through him as he plunged deep into Delilah and began to spurt wildly and uncontrollably. Minutes later, drained and contented, he lay still upon her as she gently caressed his face and idly ran her fingers through his straight black hair.

"Oh, honey," he murmured, "I sure am glad I came looking for you."

"And I," she whispered in his ear, "am glad that you found me."

He sighed and withdrew from her. He flopped down on his back beside her with his eyes closed. "With you, every time is better and better." He drew a deep breath and stretched. "Hey, what—" His eyes snapped open and he looked down in order to discover what it was that had just sent a tingling sensation through his shaft, which was lolling limply across his hard left thigh.

Delilah, lying on her side, her chin propped up in one hand, was teasing him with her peacock feather, which she had retrieved from the table beside the bed.

"It's tuckered," he told her.

"Is it?" Delilah winked at him. The tip of her peacock feather touched the tip of his shaft, and Cimarron's skin rippled because of the pleasant sensation the feather brought him. He watched as Delilah slid the feather under his shaft in an effort to raise it.

"It's far too heavy for that," he told her.

She substituted her fingers for the feather and he, already nearly stiff as a result of her earlier ministrations, quickly became hard as a rock as her hot hand continued to stroke him.

Suddenly, she was up and astride him. She eased his shaft into her and began to ride it, her pelvis rising and falling in a rhythm that Cimarron found as delightfully maddening as it was decidedly arousing. Her palms pressed against his shoulders, and as she began to swivel her pelvis, he threw back his head, closed his eyes, and moaned. His fingers dug into the bedspread as he felt the hot flood tide rising within him and then . . .

Just as he was about to explode, Delilah, with the skill of an erotic torturer, stopped moving.

"Oh, honey," he murmured as he began to slide back down from the heights to which she had just taken him.

She stirred. Began to swivel her hips again. To rise. To fall.

He felt the fire within him began to burn again and again Delilah fanned its flames with exquisite skill until the raging conflagration within him shot upward and into her. She tightened her hold on him as several spasms racked her body, and then she let out a cry that was almost savage as she, too, climaxed.

Later, as they lay side by side on the bed, they talked of everything and nothing until finally Delilah, with a sigh, said, "I guess I really should be getting back to Edwin."

"I'll walk you back to the fair, if you like," Cimarron proposed, and Delilah enthusiastically accepted his offer.

They dressed, embraced, kissed, and then left the hotel room hand in hand.

Downstairs, after Cimarron had paid the still-smirking desk clerk for the room, they left the hotel.

"Let's go this way," Delilah suggested, pointing to the right. "It's a shortcut."

"You're in a hurry to get back to your beau, are you?"

"No, I most decidedly am not, and he's a friend, not my beau. It's just that I feel guilty about deserting him the awful way I did. And the fact that I had such a good time with you makes me feel *twice* as guilty for having done so." Delilah took Cimarron's hand and led him down a side street.

They were almost at the edge of town when he let go of her hand and halted to stare intently at a poster that was nailed to a barn door.

"What is it?" she asked, turning around to face him.

"Well, I'll be damned," he muttered under his breath.

She rejoined him. "Oh, my goodness!" she cried, pointing at the poster. "That's—they're—"

"Simkins," Cimarron muttered. "And Prendergast. They're up to their old tricks, looks like."

"They're having another horse race," Delilah declared as she hurriedly read the poster. "This time right here in Gibson Station, the same as they did days ago down in Muskogee."

"And just like before," Cimarron stated, "it says right there that Simkins is claiming he'll split a five-hundred-dollar stake among the owners of the horses in the race, including his own, which his confederate Prendergast is going to ride like he did last time. Well, this time's not going to be one bit like the last time if I have anything to say or do about it!"

"What are you going to do?"

"I'm going to get back my twenty dollars that Simkins ran off with down in Muskogee and I'm going to put both him and his partner, Prendergast, in jail on a charge of larceny on account of how they ran off with all the Muskogee bettors' money plus the five-hundred-dollar stake that was supposed to be split up nice and even."

"Oh, Cimarron, forget about the twenty dollars you lost," Delilah pleaded. "Both those men may be armed. And there are two—maybe more that we don't know about—and only one of you!"

"I'd best get strutting if I'm to lay my paws on those two jaspers," Cimarron remarked as if he had heard nothing of what Delilah had just said to him. He glanced up at the sky. "The poster says the stakes race is to take place this evening at six, and by the looks of where the sun's at I'd say it's not much shy of that time right now. You stay here in town, honey, so you'll be safe should any shooting start."

He quickly kissed Delilah good-bye and then sprinted down the street to the fairgrounds, his right hand on the butt of his six-gun.

2

Cimarron ran in a kind of rolling gait, his long-legged body moving easily and lithely, the straight black hair that covered his neck and ears fluttering out behind him. The sun glinted in his emerald eyes, which seemed to see everything and miss nothing.

He was a tall man, broad in the shoulder and lean in the waist and hips, and he ran like one of the big cats pursuing its prey—with sinewy grace and many-muscled strength—not seeming to hurry and yet covering great distances with little apparent effort.

His face, sun-bronzed and weather-battered, had a raw-boned look about it, the result of a narrow nose, thin lips, and slightly sunken cheeks beneath twin ridges of prominent cheekbones. There were crow's feet at the corners of his eyes. His forehead was heavily lined and there was a deep cleft in his square chin.

A scar—a livid lifeless line of flesh—ran along the left side of his face, beginning just below his eye and stopping just above his upper lip. When he smiled, that scar gave him a sardonic look. When he frowned, it made him look menacing.

He wore a black flannel shirt beneath his buckskin jacket, faded jeans starting to fray at the knees and at the spot where his hip holster rested against his thigh, dusty black army boots worn down at the heels, a sweat-stiffened blue bandanna tied around the tautly corded column of his neck, and a black slouch hat that shadowed his face and eyes. His right hand remained on the butt of his .44 Frontier Colt as he ran on.

When he reached the fairgrounds, he found that the stakes race was just about to begin. Over the heads of the townspeople lining the dirt racetrack between the fairgrounds and the Katy depot, he spotted Prendergast aboard the horse the man had ridden in the stakes race he and his partner recently held in Muskogee. Beyond him was another man, mounted and ready for what was obviously going to be a two-rider race.

He scanned the crowd, searching for Simkins, but the man was nowhere in sight. He strode up to one of the men standing near the starting line and asked, "Where's the stakeholder? I got some bucks that are burning a hole in my pocket and I'd like to lay down a bet on this race."

"Mister Simkins is gone," replied the man without taking his avid eyes away from the horses and the starter, who was holding a pistol aimed at the sky.

"Gone where?"

"Miller's Feed and Grain in town. That's where the payoff's to be made after the race, Mister Simkins told us."

"I'm obliged to you." Cimarron turned and headed back to town, thinking as he went that Simkins and Prendergast were operating here in exactly the same manner that they had operated in Muskogee. Got to get my hands on Simkins before that race ends and Prendergast has a chance to make his getaway, he thought. But I'll have a little bit of time after the race is over to nab him on account of Prendergast'll no doubt give one of his flowery speeches. He'll praise his competition just like he did in Muskogee, so as to keep the bettors from hightailing it after Simkins before the man has had a chance to ride out of town with the bettors' money.

Cimarron loped down Gibson Station's main street, his eyes darting in every direction. He spotted Miller's Feed and Grain up ahead, but he doubted he'd find Simkins there. He knew from his recent experience with the man in Muskogee that Simkins had absolutely no intention of meeting Gibson Station's winning bettors there to pay them off any more than he had met with the Muskogee bettors after the race.

But he nevertheless veered from his path, and when he reached the entrance to Miller's, he peered inside and then yelled to the clerk behind the counter, "You got a fellow name of Simkins in here who's the stakeholder for the race out at the fairgrounds?"

The clerk shook his head. "Haven't seen the man."

Cimarron returned to the street, hesitated a moment, and then went charging across it at an angle, heading for the livery stable. Simkins has got to have a horse to get away on, he thought as he ran. There's a chance he housed it at the livery here in town while he was up to no good out there at the fairgrounds.

When he arrived at the livery, he bounded inside, hand again on his gun butt, and was about to yell for the farrier when he heard voices coming from a tack shed adjoining the livery. He made his way to its door and listened.

"But you can't leave now, Mister Simkins. You're supposed to meet with the winning bettors over at Miller's Feed and Grain."

"I told you I want my horse, and I want it now," Simkins countered.

"No, sir, I'm not turning your horse over to you. Not till after the money that's been won's been paid out to them that won it!"

"Why, you—"

Cimarron stepped into the tack shed, gun drawn and at full cock. "Stand aside, Simkins," he ordered, and Simkins, who had been about to throw a punch at the leather-aproned farrier, froze and then turned slowly around.

"This matter is none of your affair, mister, whoever you may be," Simkins said stonily. "May I suggest you mind your own business?"

"It is my business I'm minding," Cimarron calmly declared in a mild voice, "though I may be about it a bit tardily. So you're dead wrong, Simkins, when you claim that this—that you and your partner, Prendergast, are none of my affair."

Simkins' eyes narrowed as he stared uneasily at Cimarron. "Who are you?"

"You don't remember me? Now, that's a shame, on account of I remember you real well. I remember how you and Prendergast ran off with the bettors' money down in Muskogee, where you staged a stakes race just like the one that's being run out at the fairgrounds right this minute."

"You're that deputy marshal," Simkins breathed, his eyes widening as he continued to stare at Cimarron. "The one who rode that woman's horse."

Cimarron nodded. "The horse was named Fleet of Foot and he beat your Prince Charming by nigh on to a country mile. The woman's name was Miss Serena Farthing."

Simkins blinked owlishly several times and then the muscles of his rigidly set face melted into an ingratiating smile. When he spoke to Cimarron, his tone was weak and wheedling. "You have me wrong, sir. In fact, you have badly misjudged me. I had to depart Muskogee on urgent business immediately following the race, and I did so without leaving word with anyone. An unfortunate omission, I admit. But—and this is the important point that must be understood by all and sundry—although I have not yet had the opportunity to return to Muskogee to make good on my many outstanding obligations to its citizens, I do fully intend to return, at which time I shall be pleased to—"

Cimarron interrupted by tsk-tsking. "Simkins, if you could shovel shit as skillful as you lie, you could real easy make a manure pile a mile or two high."

Simkins began to splutter and insist that he was a much misunderstood—indeed, maligned—man.

Cimarron held out his left hand, palm up. "I want the

27

money you're holding. I want the tally book where you write down the names of bettors and how much they bet."

"This is highway robbery," Simkins protested.

Cimarron ostentatiously raised his .44 until it was aimed at Simkins' forehead.

Simkins hurriedly stripped off a money belt he was wearing. Then, just as quickly, he took a tally book from his hip pocket. He handed both items to Cimarron, who pocketed the book and then fastened the money belt around his waist. "Would you be willing to lend the law a hand," he asked the farrier, "and keep this jasper locked up here in your tack shed till I can get my paws on his partner and then come on back here for him?"

"Sure I will," the farrier exclaimed. "I'll be glad to cooperate with you. Lawman, the sportsmen of Gibson Town owe you a favor for what you've done here today."

"My job's but half-done, though," Cimarron said, and then left the livery. He sprinted back to the fairgrounds, and when he arrived there, he discovered that another race was about to be run. "What's going on?" he asked one of the spectators. "I thought there was only supposed to be one run for the money."

"That's right, there was," the man he had spoken to responded. "But the first race ended in a dead heat so they're going to give it another go."

Cimarron, his thumbs hooked in his cartridge belt, stood and watched Prendergast and the other rider as they approached the starting line. When the starter fired his pistol, he continued watching until the race ended and Prendergast, still sitting his saddle, proceeded to volubly and at great length praise the other rider, who had won the race. He shouldered his way through the crowd of people who were politely listening to Prendergast, although it was apparent that many of them were eager to be off to Miller's Feed and Grain to collect their winnings from Simkins.

He emerged from the crowd and walked toward Prendergast. His six-gun cleared leather. "Throw down that sidearm of yours," he ordered.

Prendergast gave him a startled glance. "What—"

"I've got your partner penned up in the livery from where he was about to ride out with the money some of these folks bet on your race. Now do like I said."

"What's going on here?" the starter yelled, making his way through the crowd toward Cimarron.

As Cimarron told the starter and the rest of the people in the watching and listening crowd about Prendergast's scheme, the man, with apparent reluctance, unleathered his gun and dropped it to the ground.

"You mean to say, sir, that Mister Simkins and Mister Prendergast here intended to abscond with our money?" the shocked starter asked when Cimarron fell silent.

"That's right," Cimarron answered. "That's exactly what I do mean. But if you folks'll follow me back to town, I'll be glad to see to it that you each get back the money you bet."

"Let's go, everybody," cried the starter, beckoning to the crowd.

As the starter turned back to town at the head of a noisy procession, Cimarron gestured with his gun and Prendergast sullenly moved his horse out in the same direction.

But even before they reached the Katy's depot, Prendergast suddenly slammed spurs to his horse, causing the animal to bolt into the crowd of people that was heading back to town.

Cimarron swore and was about to fire to wound Prendergast when the man bent down and scooped up a slender woman who began to scream and kick as he threw her over his horse's withers. Holding the woman down with one hand, Prendergast drew a Smith & Wesson .44 cavalry revolver he had hidden in a shoulder holster and fired two shots over the heads of the people in the crowd who were scattering in every direction.

"Don't you come a single step closer, lawdog," he yelled over his shoulder at Cimarron. "If you do, I'll shoot one or two of these townies just like they were turkeys and Christmas was coming."

Cimarron halted, still swearing under his breath.

"Don't come after me, lawdog," Prendergast bellowed. "If you do, I'll kill the little lady who's going to be keeping me company."

The woman lying across the horse's withers screamed even more loudly and kicked even more wildly.

Prendergast, giggling shrilly now, put rowels to his horse's flanks, and Cimarron was forced to watch him go galloping away in a northerly direction, the woman he had abducted still screaming and still kicking.

Then, as Cimarron spun around and went sprinting toward the Katy's depot, her screams grew faint and soon he could hear them no longer. He angrily leathered his gun as he passed the depot and then ran down Gibson Station's main street, heading back to the livery stable.

"Did you catch him?" asked the farrier, looking up from his hot forge, where he was hammering out a horseshoe, as Cimarron bounded into the livery.

"He got away from me," Cimarron replied, and moved to the stall where his bay stood munching hay. He had the animal saddled and bridled within minutes. After paying the farrier what he owed, he led the horse outside, boarded it, and went galloping out of town before heading north, the direction Prendergast had taken.

The level of the land rose gradually as he rode on, lashing the bay with his reins and heeling it hard. His eyes easily spotted the deep prints of Prendergast's mount in the moist ground of the sunless forest through which he was riding.

Prendergast had left a plain trail and Cimarron continued following it at a fast gallop for another few miles. It wasn't long before he caught his first glimpse of Prendergast and the man's hostage far ahead of him.

Cimarron went for his gun, but his hand halted halfway to it. Instead of drawing his .44, he turned the bay and rode northwest at a sharp angle from the trail he had been following. Although his horse was already beginning to blow and its body was lathered with sweat, he continued spurring it and lashing it with his reins.

The animal responded with a fresh burst of speed, and

within ten minutes Cimarron decided it was safe to turn the animal. He headed due east, and after riding for some time, he drew rein, slid out of the saddle, and tethered his mount to a white birch. Then, unleathering his gun, he continued heading east on foot, running as fast as he could, hoping to outdistance his quarry and then simply wait for the man to put in an appearance.

But maybe, he thought, Prendergast has gone and changed course on me. He knelt down, put an ear to the ground, and listened. A smile crept over his face as he heard the muted thunder that seemed to rumble up out of the heart of the earth—thunder that he knew was caused by horse's hooves.

He looked around him and then quickly scrambled up on top of a rocky ledge that overlooked a sparsely treed area sprinkled with sprigs of Indian rice grass. He drew his .44 and crouched on his miniature mesa, eager for his first glimpse of Prendergast.

Less than five minutes later, Prendergast rode into sight, curving in and out among the trees. As he came closer, Cimarron could hear the man cursing the woman he had taken as hostage. He saw Prendergast raise his left fist and bring it down on the back of the woman's head. But the cruel blow failed to silence her.

Cimarron tensed as Prendergast rode closer to his position, and then, just as his quarry was about to pass directly below the ledge, he leapt from it.

As his body struck Prendergast's, his left arm went around the man's neck. Both of them fell to the ground. Prendergast's horse galloped on and then halted and shook itself, causing the woman Prendergast had abducted to fall to the ground.

As he and Cimarron rolled over and over on the rocky ground, Prendergast struggled to free himself but failed in his attempt. Both men struck a sharp outcropping of shale, and Cimarron scrambled to his feet, hauling Prendergast up with him. He released his grip on the man's neck and unholstered Prendergast's .44, which he threw into a distant clump of stunted sycamores.

He thrust Prendergast away from him, and then, as the man stood there wordlessly glaring at him, he gestured, pointing to Prendergast's horse. "Go get your mount so we can all start back down the mountain."

Grumbling, Prendergast did as he was told. Cimarron, following him, yelled to the woman to get away from Prendergast's horse. She obediently scurried away from it, her hair, which had become unpinned flying out behind her.

Cimarron gave her a brief glance, noting her bruised right cheek and the fact that she had begun to cry. She's no doubt in need of comforting after her awful ordeal, he thought, hope flaring within him. She's some lovely little lady. Maybe later I can provide her with the comfort she looks to be so badly in need of.

"Climb up on that horse," Cimarron ordered Prendergast. "We're going over into the woods aways to where I left my mount."

As Prendergast put his left foot in his left stirrup, the woman suddenly came running up behind Cimarron and threw her arms around his neck.

"Oh, thank you, sir, whoever you may be," she cried, and squeezed his neck so hard he almost gagged.

As the woman continued holding tightly to Cimarron, Prendergast swiftly turned, swung one hard fist, and succeeded in knocking the gun from Cimarron's hand. Then, as Cimarron tore the woman's hands from around his neck, Prendergast kicked out viciously and the heel of his right boot slammed squarely into Cimarron's groin.

Cimarron let out a howl and doubled over as pain exploded within him, a pain so sharp and so piercing that it seemed to him like a thousand sharp knives slicing away at him. He clutched his savaged genitals and continued howling, barely aware of the fact that, when he had doubled over, the woman had lost her grip on him and fallen to the ground behind him.

Prendergast lunged at him and Cimarron, still clutching his genitals but silent now, lurched to one side. Prendergast's hands closed only on air. Cimarron thrust out his

32

right hand, reaching for his dropped gun. But Prendergast kicked the gun out of his reach and then drew back his foot, intending to kick Cimarron a second time. As the man's boot came flying toward his face, Cimarron reached out with both hands, seized the boot, and twisted it sharply.

Prendergast lost his balance and crashed to the ground. A moment later he managed to get his hands on Cimarron's six-gun. He took aim at Cimarron and fired, but just before the gun spat flame and then smoke, Cimarron again twisted Prendergast's ankle as hard as he could and the man's shot went wild. Prendergast shrieked in agony and continued shrieking even when Cimarron released him, sprang to his feet, and seized the wrist of Prendergast's gun hand in both of his hands. He slammed Prendergast's hand against a sharp outcropping of shale and then repeated the gesture twice more until Prendergast finally let go of his gun and it fell to the ground.

He released Prendergast and picked up his gun, which the man had dropped. "Get up!" he ordered.

Prendergast, his upper body propped up on his elbows, glared up at Cimarron and then slowly obeyed his order. The two men stood facing each other for a moment, neither of them speaking, both of them wearing angry expressions, and then Cimarron ordered Prendergast to move out.

Before he could do so, the woman again ran up to Cimarron, a broad smile on her face, and placed herself directly between him and Prendergast.

"You were wonderful," she told him. "So brave and manly and—"

Cimarron quickly reached out to push her aside but Prendergast suddenly seized her from behind and pulled her body back against his own.

"Let her go, Prendergast," Cimarron snapped.

"Why the hell should I, lawdog? So you can shoot me?" Prendergast hurriedly backed away from Cimarron, dragging with him the woman, who seemed to have been startled speechless. He kept her body pressed against his own so that he would not present a target for Cimarron's gun. "You try taking me," he taunted, "and you'll have to shoot straight through the lady!"

Cimarron knew what Prendergast intended to do. He's heading for that clump of sycamores to get his gun which I threw in there, he thought. But he's not got it yet.

"What the hell have you got to grin about, lawdog?" Prendergast shrilled at him.

Cimarron holstered his gun and then ran toward Prendergast and his hostage.

Prendergast, his eyes wide with alarm when he realized his plan had failed, shoved the woman in Cimarron's direction and then turned and raced toward the sycamores.

The woman, her arms akimbo and stumbling badly, and the advancing Cimarron collided. Both of them fell to the ground. But Cimarron, unlike the woman, didn't remain down. In seconds, he was up and racing after Prendergast. The distance between them narrowed and then Prendergast was in among the sycamores and frantically searching the sun-dappled ground for his gun.

He found it just as Cimarron came crashing through the undergrowth toward him. He turned, dropped down on one knee, eared back the hammer of his weapon, and fired at Cimarron.

But his target anticipated the shot and swerved just in time to avoid the bullet. Cimarron continued zigzagging through the trees as Prendergast fanned the hammer of his gun, firing wildly at the lawman, who was now here, now there, never in the place he had been only an instant earlier.

Cimarron suddenly stumbled and fell over a half-buried sycamore root. His head hit the base of the tree and he almost lost consciousness. Through a bright-red mist that badly clouded his vision, he saw someone coming toward him: Prendergast. Heard someone—Prendergast—laughing gaily. Looked up and saw the gun in Prendergast's two hands, its barrel angling down toward him.

He lurched to the side, unleathered his gun, rolled over, and fired a split second after Prendergast did. Prendergast's bullet plowed harmlessly into the dank ground. Cimarron's plowed harmfully into the right side of Prendergast's skull. It left a small round hole that quickly became wet with black blood.

Lying on his belly, his gun held in both hands and still aimed upward at his prisoner, Cimarron was breathing heavily as he kept his eyes on Prendergast's face, which wore an expression first of puzzled surprise and then of utter defeat. He continued watching as Prendergast's eyes rolled slowly upward until only the whites were visible. He watched Prendergast's knees buckle and then bend and the gun slip from the dying man's fingers. He watched, his own expression grim, as Prendergast crumpled to the ground, where he lay in a lifeless heap among the dead leaves and the dirt.

"Marshal?"

Cimarron heard the woman's tentative call, heard the fear that lurked behind the sound. He got up, eased back the hammer of his Colt, leathered the gun, and sighed. He left the shelter of the sycamore grove, and as he did so, the woman whimpered wordlessly, her hands clasped just below her breasts, her posture rigid in the distance.

"It's done with," he told her in a flat tone of voice. "He's dead."

"You killed him?"

"I killed him."

She ran to him then, asking how, asking if he was sure Prendergast was dead—"truly dead" was the way she put it—and he, vaguely sickened as he always was when he had been forced to kill a man, answered her shortly and sharply and then told her that she was a damn fool for what she had done. "You could've got yourself killed," he snarled at her. "You could've got us both killed!" The anger welling up in him, the bitter fruit of the deed he had just done under the leafy canopy of the sycamores, made him turn his back on her. She was, he knew, merely a convenient if improper target for his fury. He bluntly ordered her to mount Prendergast's horse: the three of them were heading back to Gibson Station.

As they rode in silence, Cimarron's anger dulled to a dark gloom. The woman avoided looking at him, and by the time they arrived back in Gibson Station, darkness had fallen. He asked her where the town's coroner could be found. After telling him in a cold voice, she dismounted, handed him the reins of Prendergast's horse, and flounced haughtily away from him with no farewell or backward glance.

He watched her go and then, following her directions, made his way to the coroner's office, where he turned Prendergast's gun and horse over to the man along with Prendergast's body, which he had brought into town draped over his horse's withers. He explained who he was and what had happened.

"They," he told the coroner, referring to the horse and gun, "ought, I reckon, to pay for a boot-hill burial."

"They will indeed, Deputy," declared the coroner. "What shall I do with the money that's left over after I sell off the dear departed's possessions? Will you come back to collect it?"

Cimarron, heading for the door, shook his head. "Donate it to your town's widows' and orphans' fund, if you've got one. If you've not, set one up."

As he emerged from the coroner's office, Cimarron spotted the wagonload of prisoners across the street and the familiar face of the man guarding them. Dodging through the street's heavy traffic, he made his way over to the prisoners' guard. "Howdy, Henry! Long time no see."

"Well, I do declare! It's you, Cimarron! How the hell are you, old son? I haven't laid eyes on you—what's it been—months now, right?"

"How've you been keeping, Henry?"

"Tolerable, Cimarron, tolerable, though I've got rheumatism in my knees and sometimes it flares up real fierce on me. I guess I'm getting way too old to be out here chasing up and down the owlhoot trail after the likes of those jaspers"—Henry pointed to the sullen and surly prisoners who were all handcuffed and seated in the wagon bed. "I ought to be home with my missus, not out here in

36

the Territory, where, for deputies like us, there's neither peace of mind nor much likelihood of ever dying in bed."

"Henry, were you to retire to a rocker, you'd either rust or rot, one or the other, and you damn well know it. Keeping company with the snakes that infest the Territory, human and otherwise, it's what keeps you from caving in or falling all to pieces."

Henry grinned. "Why do we do it, Cimarron? They kill us off like flies. We don't get paid a decent wage. We're out in all kinds of weather and we don't get to see much of our loved ones. Why in the name of all that's sane and sensible, Cimarron, do men like you and me do like we do out here in the Territory, year in and year out?"

"Some men, Henry, they fall prey to demon rum. Others to laudanum or cocaine. With us, our vice is star-packing. It gets a strong grip on a man after a while and won't let go, lawdogging does."

"I reckon you're right, Cimarron. What are you doing here in Gibson Station?"

Cimarron told him. "You driving alone, are you, Henry?"

"No. There's three other deputies with me. Two green-horns and Will Haley. You know Will, don't you?" When Cimarron nodded, Henry continued, "They're all out at the fairgrounds. The four of us came by here hoping to see the stakes race we heard was to be run here today, but it was all over and done with by the time we got here.

"We're taking turns standing guard. One of us guards the prisoners while the other three go to the fair."

"I was out there myself earlier today. Had me a ride on that merry-go-round they got."

"You don't get enough of straddling a saddle, you have to pay to ride one of those painted ponies?"

Cimarron matched Henry's grin.

"Me, I had the time of my life just before it got dark. I had my fortune told, Cimarron."

"You what?"

"Sure enough, I did. By a gypsy woman who's got a tent set up out at the fairgrounds. Cost me a whole dollar, too, to hear what's in store for me."

"I didn't see any gypsy woman or fortune-telling tent out at the fairgrounds when I was there."

"The gypsies pulled in just before it turned dark," Henry sighed. "You should have seen her, that gypsy woman, Cimarron. Dark she was. Wild-looking. I couldn't take my eyes off her, nor my mind neither, ever since I first spotted her. She's a woman born to turn the head of any man she meets, she is. When she took my hand in hers— hell, Cimarron, my heart hasn't palpitated like it did then since I last visited Madame Morrissey's parlor house up in Tulsey Town."

When he paused, Cimarron said, "Be seeing you, Henry."

"Hey, where are you off to so all of a sudden?"

"Got some important business to take care of."

First of all, Cimarron thought, heading for the livery, I've got to turn over the money I took off Simkins to somebody trustworthy so's they can turn it back to the ones who bet it on the race.

At the livery he spoke to the farrier. "I'm obliged to you for holding on to Simkins for me. I've come to take him off your hands."

Just before Cimarron left the livery with his prisoner, he told the farrier, "I'm going to turn the money folks bet on that crooked race over to the Lighthorse police here in town. They'll be returning it to the ones it belongs to. Spread the word, will you?"

"I will, Deputy."

Cimarron bade the farrier good-bye and marched Simkins to the town jail, where he turned him over to the Creek Lighthorseman in charge, who promptly placed the man in a cell.

He explained to the Indian lawman about the money that was to be returned to Gibson Station's bettors and handed him Simkins' tally book. After counting the money contained in the money belt, he said, "Twenty dollars of this is mine. I bet it in Muskogee some days back, on the same kind of crooked race Simkins and Prendergast staged down here. The rest of the money—maybe you'll see to it that it gets to Muskogee so the folks there can get back what's rightly theirs. Any that's left over, well, tell them they can do with it what they think's fit."

"I'll take care of it," the Lighthorseman promised and then, as Cimarron headed for the door, asked, "When will you be back for your prisoners?"

"Soon. After I've had my fortune told by a gypsy lady out at the fairgrounds." That gypsy fortune-teller might be able to tell me something about Mala and Serena's money, he added to himself.

He left the jail and returned to the fairgrounds, where he soon found the gypsy tent standing not far from the merry-go-round. He entered it and, finding it empty, was about to call out when a yellow silk drape stirred at the rear of the tent. It was drawn aside by a sultry woman he recognized immediately.

"Howdy, Rupa."

"You know my name?" she asked, her expression stern as she stared at Cimarron. And then she nodded knowingly. "Ah, it is the *gajo* from Three Forks."

"Three Forks was where we met, all right. But I'm not from there. I just happened to be passing through that day when we ran into each other."

"You have come here to have your fortune told?"

"I have."

"Sit down." Rupa indicated the square table standing between them, which was covered with a blue satin cloth on which yellow moons were embroidered.

Cimarron sat down at it and Rupa seated herself across from him.

"One dollar."

He dug down in his pocket, came up with the money, and handed it to her. It quickly disappeared into a pocket of her bright magenta skirt. She leaned over the table toward him, and his eyes dropped to the provocative cleavage that her purple blouse revealed. "Give me your hand."

He gave it to her, thinking, That's not all I'd like to give such a lovely-looking lady like yourself. As Rupa studied his palm, Cimarron studied her, noting again, as he had the first and only other time they had met on the trail, her glossy black hair bound in a single braid; her equally black eyes, which seemed to glow with an inner light; her tawny skin, nearly as dark as tanbark; her perfectly formed lips; and her long black eyelashes. His eyes dropped again to her rounded bosom, as rounded, he remembered, as her hips, which he could not now see because they were hidden beneath the tabletop. Altogether, he thought approvingly, this Rupa is a handsome example of womanhood.

"You have a long life line," she told him, her head lowered, her eyes intently gazing at his upturned palm. "But it is bent in some places, nearly broken in other places. You must take care. For you, danger lurks in the future. Should you fail to remain alert, it will pounce and . . . See here?"

"See where?"

Rupa's finger touched a point on his palm. "Here your life line is ragged. Beware of men with guns."

"I'm always wary of such jaspers," he told her, amused and thinking that any man with an ounce of sense was always cautious of armed men. What she had told him, he realized, could apply to anyone.

"You have known much love in your life," Rupa remarked. "You will know much more. You are a man blessed with the love of many women." She looked up at him. "It is true?"

"You sure are a clever lady," he told her solemnly. "Now, how in the world did you know that about me?"

"It is written plainly in your palm." She touched a small crease in his palm. "But you must be careful where the ladies are concerned. I see here that there is a woman. She will break your heart."

"How?"

Rupa leaned over and peered at Cimarron's palm. "It is not clear how she will do it, only that she will do it. Ah!" she suddenly exclaimed, and drew back. "Your heart—I see that it has been broken already. But not only by a woman. By a woman and someone"—she examined his palm carefully—"someone small. A child?"

40

Cimarron closed his eyes for a moment. Then, opening them again, he said, "Her name was Lilah. The child—he was my son. They died." He stared intently at Rupa and wondered how she could have known about Lilah and the baby. Or had it been merely a guess on her part that had landed randomly on target?

"Lilah loved you."

"I was lucky. She did."

"Hold up your hand," Rupa directed. "Like this." She held up her own hand, her fingers widely separated. Cimarron did as she had asked and she declared, "You will soon know much trouble. And much danger."

"How'd you figure that out?"

Rupa pointed to his upraised hand. "The angle formed by your left thumb and your index finger, we gypsies call it 'the devil's saddle.' See how wide it is on your hand? You will have much misfortune soon."

Again Cimarron found himself thinking that what she had just told him could apply to almost anyone at any time.

"But all is not dark in your future," Rupa continued. "You will have some good luck too—perhaps much good luck. You have a long index finger, which is the digit of good fortune."

She looked up at Cimarron and a smile flickered across her face. "You told Luluvo when you talked to him at Three Forks that you were a lawman, as I recall."

"You recall correct. I'm a deputy marshal."

"But one who has done some thieving in his time, eh?"

Startled, Cimarron lowered his hand. "How'd you figure that out about me?"

"We gypsies call the little finger 'the magpie.' The magpie, as you probably know, is first and foremost a thieving bird. See how your 'magpie' twists and turns in places? It tells me that you are—or perhaps have been—a thief."

Cimarron darted a surreptitious glance at his little finger, which had apparently betrayed to Rupa the fact that he had, for years before becoming a deputy marshal, lived the life of a road agent.

"For another dollar," Rupa said, "I will tell you more."

"I've heard plenty. More than enough to hold me for a while. I think I'd best quit while I'm ahead . . . if I am ahead."

She gave him an amused look.

"I've got a question for you before I go, Rupa. Do you know a lady, a gypsy lady, who no doubt has a real long little finger since she's a thief if ever there was one—name of Mala?"

"Mala?"

Cimarron proceeded to tell Rupa about the scheme the gypsy woman named Mala had practiced on Serena Farthing in Muskogee to bilk her out of her savings.

"I know Mala," Rupa volunteered when he had finished his account of the Serena-Mala matter. "She is not of our tribe, the Lowara. She is a member of the Tshurara tribe, notorious thieves and troublemakers. The Tshurara give all gypsies a bad name."

"Would you by any chance happen to know where I might find her?"

"We gypsies, as Luluvo told you when you met us on the trail at Three Forks, are roamers like the wind. We seldom stay in one place for very long. But I have heard—" Rupa fell silent and gave Cimarron a speculative glance.

"You've heard?" he prodded.

"The Tshurara, it is rumored, have gone to Salina on the Grand River in Cherokee Nation to make their winter camp. November is almost here. Soon the snow will fly. Many gypsies settle down for the winter. You may find the Tshurara—Mala—there."

"I'm obliged to you, Rupa, for the information." Cimarron rose. "If I get up that way before spring, I'll see if I can't lay my hands on Mala and maybe get my lady friend's money back."

Rupa remained seated and silent.

Cimarron touched the brim of his hat to her and then left the tent. He made his way back to town, thinking as he went that without five prisoners to herd east to Fort Smith, he could easily make the trip up to Salina, and that if he did get Serena's money back from Mala for her, she'd be mighty grateful, which meant . . . He smiled.

His smile broadened as he rounded the Katy depot, where lighted lanterns hung like bright orange eyes in the black night, and he spotted the wagon that was pulling out of town. "Pull up, Henry," he yelled to the deputy driving the wagon loaded with prisoners and three other deputies.

" 'Evening, Cimarron," Henry called out. "Boys, look at who's here. It's Cimarron. I told you I run into him in town today."

Greetings were exchanged between Cimarron and the other deputies, and then he asked them if they'd be willing to take his five prisoners back to Fort Smith along with their own.

"Sure, we'll take them," Henry volunteered amiably. "Where are they?"

"In town. In the jail there. I've got receipts for all of them." He pulled the receipts from his pocket and handed them to Henry. "You can hand those receipts over to the Lighthorseman in charge of the jail and he'll turn my prisoners over to you."

"We'll do it," Henry said. "But I'm wondering how come you don't want to take them back to Fort Smith yourself."

"I've got other fish to fry," Cimarron answered. "I'm going to try to trap me a gypsy lady who has the nasty habit of tricking honest folks out of their life's savings."

3

After spending the night in Gibson Station's hotel, Cimarron left town the next morning aboard the Katy railroad, heading north into Cherokee Nation.

He arrived at Pryor Creek in the early afternoon, and after unloading his bay, which had traveled on a flatcar sided with pine slats, he walked the horse to the town's livery stable where he stalled it and paid for a mix of corn and oats which he placed in the stall's feed bin before proceeding to unsaddle the animal.

"Shit," he muttered as he removed his saddle blanket and saw the puffed muscles ridging the bay's back.

"What's wrong, mister?" inquired the stableboy who was rubbing down a gelding in an adjoining stall.

"My mount's sweat-scalded. Which means I'll be obliged to leave him here for a day, maybe two, till his hurting heals, before I dare ride him again. You got any ground-up pumice stone, boy?"

Later, when the stableboy had given him an earthen-ware crock containing ground pumice, Cimarron proceeded to sprinkle the substance on the bay's injured back. Using part of his saddle blanket, he smoothed the powder over the swollen muscles. Then, leaving the stall and turning to the stableboy, he said, "I'll be needing a good saddle horse. You got any that's for rent?"

"Two. One's not much more'n crowbait. But the other's sturdy enough."

The stableboy showed Cimarron the two horses he had spoken of, and Cimarron chose the big-brisketed black the stableboy recommended.

"I'd be much obliged to you," he told the stableboy, "if, while I'm away, you'd be sure to keep my horse well-watered and grained. You do all that, and there's a dollar in my pocket that'll wind up in yours once I get back from Salina."

"That's where you're headed, mister? Salina?"

Cimarron nodded as he shook out his saddle blanket to air it and then folded it and placed it on the black's back.

"You got folks there? A lady friend maybe?"

"Nope. Neither. I'm on the trail of some gypsies."

"So's a lot of folks these days, it seems."

Cimarron, as he cinched his saddle in place on the black, glanced at the stableboy. "What might you mean by that?"

"Nothing. Just that there were some gypsies passing through town a while back, and when they were gone, so were a whole lot of Miz Calhoun's white leghorn layers. Her man and some of his kin went riding out looking for the gypsies, but the scalawags weren't nowhere to be found. They'd up and disappeared just like water into parched earth."

Cimarron slid the headstall over the black's ears and a few minutes later, when he had the animal bridled, he led it out of the livery into the afternoon's bright sunshine. The yellowed leaves of a cottonwood drifted down upon him and the black as the tree's branches were stirred by an Indian-summer wind.

He stepped into the saddle and rode out of town, his gaze wandering among the women who happened to cross or parallel his path. He gave each one of them a smile and touched the brim of his hat to them. Why is it, he wondered, that so many ladies give me such sour looks when all I'm trying to be is pleasant? He looked longingly back over his shoulder at a young woman who, in response to his warm smile and respectful salute, had blushed prettily and then turned away to examine the goods on display in a window, although he doubted that she was genuinely interested in plows or in harrows either.

He sighed. Had I time to linger, he thought, who knows what might have happened between me and that little lady? We might have partaken of some ice cream someplace. She might have invited me to her place for a home-cooked meal. We might have gotten together in a nice soft bed somewhere, the two of us. He sighed again, rode out of town, and headed due east for Salina.

The sun was setting by the time he reached the Cherokee settlement that had been his destination. He entered the quiet town and dismounted in front of the first restaurant he came to. After tethering the black to a hitchrail, he entered the almost-empty restaurant and took a table near the door. He was studying the blackboard on which was chalked the day's menu, when a dark-skinned man appeared in the doorway of the kitchen and let out a whoop.

Cimarron nodded to the man, a wide smile splitting his face.

The man hurried across the room to Cimarron's table. "What brings you to Salina this time, Cimarron?" He thrust out his hand.

As the two men shook hands, Cimarron answered, "I'm fixing to do a favor for a friend. I heard, Bill, that there were some gypsies camped somewhere in the vicinity, and it's them I want to meet up with. You know anything about them?"

"Not much. A little. Listen, Cimarron, I got my only other customer's steak frying in the kitchen. When I've dished it out to him and have rustled you up some grub, I'll come back and we'll talk. What'll you have to eat?"

"A pair of fried pork chops. Some potatoes. Corn bread and coffee."

Bill rose and returned to the kitchen.

When he reappeared at Cimarron's table sometime later, he put down a plate heaped high with food. Beside it he placed utensils and a red-and-white-checkered napkin. "You want coffee now or later?"

"Later."

Bill sat down at the table and, as Cimarron hungrily forked food into his mouth, declared, "There's been some bad feeling among the other Cherokees here in town and around the area against those gypsies."

"They're here, then?"

"They've made what looks to be a pretty permanent winter camp northeast of town. It's about halfway from here to Spavinaw on the east bank of the Grand River. There's enough water and wood up there to last them quite a spell."

"Has there been anything more than just bad feelings between you Indians and those gypsies, Bill?"

"Don't go lumping me in with the rest of my people, Cimarron. I've got nothing against gypsies, nor anybody else for that matter. But to answer your question, no, there's been no fighting or anything like that, if that's what you're getting at."

"No shooting?"

"No shooting."

Several minutes later, Cimarron swallowed the last of his corn bread with which he had sopped up the juices left by his fried pork chops. The heavy meal had completely and quickly disappeared from his plate.

"What's your business with the gypsies, Cimarron?" Bill asked. "What've they done to set the law on their trail?"

Cimarron told the Cherokee about what had happened between Mala and Serena.

"Typical," Bill said when Cimarron had finished his account of the swindle. "People here in town say their children aren't safe any more than their money is with those gypsies skulking about. They steal little children, gypsies do."

"Is that a fact, Bill?"

"Well, it's what people say happens, I can tell you that much."

"I've always wondered about how some people can make

47

up outlandish notions and pass them off as pure gospel when there's often not so much as a single shred of evidence to back them up."

"You don't think gypsies steal children?"

"I've never heard of a case where they did. All I've ever heard were, like I said, notions people had in their heads about the matter."

"Well, regardless, most folks feel we Cherokees would all be better off without any gypsies around. You'll have to admit that, Cimarron. Look what one of their women did to your gullible lady friend from Muskogee."

"Oh, I'm not pretending they're simon-pure, all of them. It's just that I suspect maybe gypsies have been painted blacker'n most of them deserve. I've known a few of them in my time who worked hard as tinsmiths and tinkers out here on the frontier, that sort of thing."

"Well, I can tell you a whole lot of people would be happier if the gypsies moved far away from here. The town council is even talking about passing an ordinance against allowing any minstrels or mountebanks on our streets. And some young hotheads are starting to talk vigilante justice. There's bad blood about, Cimarron, and it's started simmering. It just might be boiling before long."

"Let's hope that cooler heads such as your own, Bill, will prevail. Now, I'll have some of your coffee if you're still making the kind a spoon'll stand straight up in."

The sun had vanished when Cimarron rode out of Salina.

He rode for some time without seeing any other rider, as the bright blue of the sky turned first to bronze and then to purple. Shadows eased out of nowhere to take possession of the land they darkened.

He rode northeast, the eastern bank of the Grand River on his left, the motion of the black beneath him steady and soothing, as the young night came alive with the chirping of crickets. The stars came out and the full moon rose to bathe the land below it in a thin white light. He dozed.

He jerked awake an unknown amount of time later when he heard the harsh sound of metal against metal and realized that someone nearby had just levered the bolt of a rifle. Ahead of him in the distance, a bonfire burned.

His hand dropped to the butt of his Colt. His eyes darted in every direction, seeking the source of the ominous sound he had just heard while simultaneously searching for cover he knew he might need, and need quickly.

There was no cover nearby, he quickly discovered, so he decided to head for the bonfire, which signaled the presence of a camp. But before he could heel his horse, a grating voice pierced the darkness, silencing the crickets.

"Hoist your hands, stranger."

Cimarron reluctantly drew rein and raised his hands.

"Step down and cool your saddle," ordered the same voice, and Cimarron obediently dismounted and stood, hands above his head, beside his horse as he peered into the night and saw only darkness.

A man armed with a carbine materialized from around the rump of his black and disarmed him. After thrusting Cimarron's .44 into his waistband, the man barked an order, and a second man appeared from the shadows to swiftly search Cimarron's pockets. A moment later, having found Cimarron's badge, the second man held it up for the man with the carbine to see, then returned it to Cimarron's pocket.

"Ah, so the one we were warned about has come," the man with the rifle solemnly declared. "It is good that we kept watch."

At that moment, Cimarron suddenly stepped to one side, seized the man who had taken and then returned his badge, and held him in front of him with both hands as he and his prisoner faced the unsmiling man with the carbine.

"I don't know why you fellows want to throw down on me," Cimarron snarled, "but I advise you to forget whatever play it was you were planning on making."

"You, an unarmed man," said the man with the carbine, "would tell us what to do? We, who inhabit the night like shadows? Shadows with many guns?"

"You'd best keep your distance, else I'll slit your friend's throat from ear to ear." As he spoke, Cimarron bent down, pulled his bowie knife from his boot, and held its blade against his captive's throat.

The man in his hands, to Cimarron's surprise, merely giggled. And then, in one sudden movement, he rammed both of his elbows into Cimarron's ribs, spun around as Cimarron gasped and lost his grip on him, and threw a punch that struck Cimarron square on the jaw and sent him reeling backward to crash into the trunk of an oak.

Cimarron, stunned, fell to the ground. Before he could regain his feet, the night burst into noisy life. Shadowy figures of men were suddenly everywhere, speaking in the language Cimarron recalled having heard used by the gypsies he had met at the Three Forks Area. It's Romany they're speaking, he thought as two men seized him and hauled him to his feet. While he struggled to free himself, the man with the carbine shouted an order and the two men holding him prisoner half-marched and half-dragged him toward the bonfire blazing in the distance.

When they reached it, they flung Cimarron to the ground in front of a covered wagon, and he realized that he was in the center of a gypsy encampment. Women with gaudy kerchiefs bound about their heads stared silently at him, children stood just as mutely by their sides. He raised himself up on his elbows, his eyes on the man with the carbine, who was cradling it almost idly in the crook of his right arm.

The man was of slender build but gave, Cimarron thought, an impression of immense strength barely kept under control. His face was dark but not as dark as those of his companions. His eyes were an odd color that might have been black or dark gray or even purple. He looks a little, Cimarron thought, like a half-starved ferret on the prowl.

"I am Kore of the Tshurara tribe of gypsies," the man announced with pride and the hint of a challenge in his resonant voice. "Are you the lawman they call Cimarron?"

Now, how the hell does this Kore, on whom I've never

50

laid so much as an eye, know my name? Cimarron wondered. "I am," he replied in response to the question. "What—"

"You have come to the camp of the Tshurara to make trouble for the Rom," Kore accused, his black eyes glinting in the light of the bonfire.

"I came hunting you folks," Cimarron declared, "on account of one of your women ran off with some money that belonged to a friend of mine down in Muskogee. The woman's name is Mala. Now, if you boys'll just let me have a talk with her—"

"We will teach you to leave the Tshurara alone," Kore interrupted. He raised his free left hand and gestured peremptorily.

As several men began to circle and then move in on him, Cimarron leapt to his feet. Instinctively, he reached for his six-gun and then remembered that it had been taken from him by Kore. His gaze dropped to the rawhide lariats that had materialized in the hands of the advancing men. There was, he saw, a honda fastened on one end of each of the lariats. He knew what the gypsies wanted to do to him. Their intent was evident in their cold eyes and in the way their hands gripped their lariats and their fingers played almost lovingly with the lengths of rawhide as they watched him, waiting for him to make a move.

He made one. He lunged for the nearest of the men, caught his target around the waist, and brought the man to the ground. As he fell on top of the man he had downed, he wrested the lariat from the man's hand and turned. Getting to his knees, he drew back his arm, the lariat clenched tightly in his fist.

But he never got a chance to use his weapon because, at that instant, one of the gypsies swung his lariat and it came whistling down, its honda striking Cimarron behind the left ear. Pain shot through his skull like a blast of buckshot, erupting from the spot where the honda had burst the flesh behind his ear. He felt it ricocheting inside his skull, saw the world around him momentarily blur. He tried to get to his feet, but another honda hit him on the forehead. Blood burst through his shattered skin and ran down into his eyes. He struck out with the lariat he still had in his hand but managed to hit no one.

The gypsies continued to beat him with their lariats, hard leather hondas savaging his head and body as he struggled to fight his way to his feet, his arms flailing. He tried to defend himself but failed to do so because pain had taken possession of his mind, and because the unrelenting succession of blows he was taking was steadily sapping the strength from his body.

He blinked several times and then tried to wipe the sweat and blood from his eyes. Hondas landed on his forearms. Lariats circled his legs, were jerked abruptly, and he was felled.

"*May mishto les o thud kata i gurumni kai tordjo!*"

Another man laughed. "Kore speaks the truth. It is easier to milk a cow that stands still. Hold him!"

Cimarron felt himself being dragged to his feet by two men. He stood there gasping, blood and sweat streaming into his eyes, and he wished, for one wild moment, that he was blind so that he could not see what was happening to him, could not feel the pain that the gypsies' lariats were bringing to every inch of his body—his chest, his arms, his legs, his head, even his groin.

He tried valiantly to break free of his captors but he could not. His head hung down helplessly. His body slumped forward. He heard voices—then scornful laughter. He felt himself melting in the hot crucible of an awful agony he could neither prevent nor avoid.

"Stay away from the Tshurara, lawman!" Kore's voice came to him as if the gypsy were miles away. "If you do not, you will die!"

They were the last words he heard, the last sounds his brain recorded, before he felt himself slipping and then rapidly sliding down into a black whirlpool, and he found himself wondering if death was awaiting him at the bottom of the swirling water's ugly vortex.

But it was not death that awaited him in the ebony

emptiness of the void in which he drifted, buffeted by bitter memories, by dead desires, by lost dreams.

He spoke her name aloud, his ma's name, but his tongue seemed rusty as it tried to form the long-unspoken vowels and consonants. He saw her in the blackness: she was reaching out to him and he was running toward her, once again the boy he had long ago so happily been, and then he was in her strong arms and did not care that the world was a dangerous place, a disappointing place, and he could smell the odors that clung to her, the odors that were such an integral part of her—earth, freshly baked bread, the sweetness of preserves imprisoned in glass under paraffin caps.

He told her of his woe whose name was Pa. Told her of the leather belt his pa had just slid from its loops and laid so severely across his bare and quivering backside. Because he had been teasing the girls again, using what his pa had called "bad and beastly" words.

"He won't let me be who I am, Ma," he wailed, and she, that strong and ever-enduring woman, ran her gnarled fingers through his long black hair and spoke of harsh things: honor, duty, chastity.

"Your pa loves you, son," she said, and he said, "No, he don't, he hates me and my ways!" And she had clucked soothingly and held his head against her breasts, and somehow his pain began to shrink until finally it disappeared altogether. "He was a hellion when he was young, your pa was," his mother whispered. "I reckon he sees his own hot blood boiling up in you, and that makes him fearful sometimes of what might befall you, boy. Don't be hard on him when he's hard on you, on account of how he don't want bad things to be your lot in life."

And then his ma was gone, lost to him in the darkness that was his life, and he was leaving the homeplace in the darkness of another night, taking only the clothes on his back and the worn work boots on his feet. When dawn came, he was miles away from the homeplace.

The years that followed his departure came and went uncounted and unchronicled by him. They marked him.

They gave him joy with one hand and took peace of mind with the other. He drifted here and there, gambled on Mississippi riverboats, drove cattle through the Nations into Kansas, narrowly avoiding being shanghaied while consorting and cavorting with the warm and wonderful women he bought, one after another, on the Barbary Coast. He killed a man in Denver who had challenged his three-card monte game, and he did hard time in the federal penitentiary for the killing despite his counselor's earnest but patently insincere plea of "mitigating circumstances" and "self-defense."

Once he had become a free man again, he drifted aimlessly and soon found himself riding with other hardcases, helping to relieve banks and trains and stagecoaches of their money.

A groan he did not recognize as having come from his own throat sounded in the darkness.

He was once again in the bank in the Texas Panhandle and he was once again hunkered down in front of the open iron safe stuffing money into a sack. Someone shouted. Something about the law and let's ride. He was turning and rising, earing back the hammer of his six-gun. The man he saw silhouetted in the doorway was wearing a nickel star. He didn't think; he fired. And then he ran past the man lying motionless on the floor, heading for the door.

Suddenly he stopped. Turned. Looked down. Recognized the man he had shot as his pa. Felt ice invade his veins. Shivered. Shouted questions at the terrified patrons of the bank and the cowering tellers.

They told him that the sheriff had come to their town after the death of his wife. That he had been a good man, a solid citizen. That they had, in time, asked him to be their sheriff. That he had consented . . .

Cimarron turned and fled from the bank. Outside, he tossed the sack full of money to one of his confederates, swung into his saddle, and ignoring the shouted questions of the men with whom he had been riding the owlhoot trail for so long, rode away.

Alone.

And alone he had been ever since, the name that once had been his abandoned. It was a Mexican woman south of the border who had first called him Cimarron. She had told him, he remembered, that the word, in Spanish, meant "wild" and "unruly." That it was used to describe a man or an animal who prefers to be alone and not a part of any pack.

The name clung to him. He learned to hide behind it.

He screamed without making a sound. Because he was there, now, his pa, his dead lips gibbering accusations, his dead eyes burning red holes in the Stygian blackness, his skeletal right index finger pointing at his son.

"Why?" wailed his dead father.

Cimarron covered his ears with both hands, but the word echoed and reechoed in the haunted chambers of his mind and he knew there was no acceptable or satisfactory answer to the awful question.

"*Why?*" wailed his dead father a second time, and Cimarron as soundlessly screamed again. And again.

He was jolted into a kind of chaotic consciousness that was characterized by sudden sharp pains in his back and right shoulder. Darkness shrouded him. He blinked, realizing he had just fallen off a horse, but the blackness still surrounded him. He rubbed his sore eyes, but still he could see absolutely nothing. He heard a horse moving nearby. His horse? The black he had rented at the livery in Salina? He did not, and could not, know because he could not see the animal or anything else in the dark world he now inhabited.

But he guessed that he had been aboard the horse that he could hear browsing near him. He guessed that he had probably been placed upon the animal after the Tshurara had beaten him into insensibility.

Where, he wondered, am I now? And why can't I see? He raised his hands to his face and felt the dried blood that had caked upon it. The bastards, he thought as pain from the many wounds made by the gypsies' leather hondas tore at him with its sharp claws. They've blinded me, he thought, gritting his teeth behind his lacerated lips.

He raised himself up on his elbows and felt the sun warm, but not yet hot, on his face. It's morning, he thought. I must have been out for hours. He struggled to his feet and stood there, his boots planted far apart for balance, swaying and on the verge of falling as his battered body protested his movements which brought him unrelenting pain.

Panic suddenly stormed through him as he stood there unsteadily and unable to see, and he wondered if he would ever know the world again in terms of its visual loveliness or if he would be condemned from now on and forever to experience it only through sound and touch. The panic he was feeling goaded him and he clawed at his swollen eyelids. He feverishly pried them apart, but still no light was visible to his wide and wildly staring eyes.

Sweating now, although the air was cool, he took a step to the right and then turned, moving off to the left, uncertain of where he was going or even why. He stumbled over a deadfall and went down, crashing into underbrush that tore at his face and body with merciless wooden fingers.

He got up cursing and floundered his way out of the tangle of undergrowth. Once clear of it, he kept moving, walking in what he believed to be a wide circle, searching for his horse. He stopped. Listened. He heard the sound of wild geese honking their way through the sky on their annual southward journey, and he remembered the sight of them—their long necks outthrust, their wings steadily and untiringly flapping, their formation a sometimes straight but more often a ragged V. He kept moving, telling himself that to do something was better than to do nothing, and minutes later, more by accident than intent, his outstretched hands collided with flesh.

He seized the mane of the horse he had come upon, and clung to it desperately, burying his face against the horse's neck. He breathed deeply, taking in the horse's strong odor of sweat, grateful to be in touch with another living, breathing creature.

His fingers fumbled over the saddle and along the worn bridle reins. His gear, he realized as his fingers blindly traced the familiar tooling. He touched the rope he knew so well that hung from his saddle horn. He spoke in a hushed voice to the horse.

It nickered and tossed its head.

And then the horse suddenly reared and his fingers were ripped free of its mane. The animal went racing away from him and he shouted at it, swore at it—all to no avail. He listened in despair to the fading sound of its hoofbeats, and soon they could no longer be heard. He was alone again in a place he did not know and could not see, alone with only his pain to keep him company.

He threw back his head and felt the sun warm on his face, and he turned, first this way, then that, until it was heating the left side of his face. Then he set out in a straight line, keeping the morning sun to his left side, heading south, his destination, Salina.

The sun was heating the right side of his face hours later when he collided with a boulder and fell facedown in the dirt, clutching his right knee, which had struck the stone. Cursing, he got up and limped on, still blind and bleeding again, a desperate man who was without a weapon or a horse in a hostile and invisible world.

Fever joined him on the trail. It marched with him as he put one leaden foot down in front of the other. It sent him warm visions of the welcoming arms of beautiful women and of huge glasses of cold foaming beer as he staggered on, thinking dully, Salina, Salina, Salina.

There'd be a doctor there, he told himself. Stop, urged Fever. He shook his head and shambled doggedly on.

In the sky above him, a turkey buzzard appeared and began to circle.

I'll get back my horse once I get safely to Salina, he thought.

And you'll ride it through the gates of hell, Fever screeched mockingly at him.

I've got to keep going, he thought.

Rest, Fever urged seductively.

He dropped to his knees and knelt on the ground, supporting himself with the knuckles of both stiff fists, his head hanging down and sweat slipping from it to make dark dots in the dust he could not see.

Painfully, he dragged himself to his feet as a thought nagged at him. There was, he knew, something he was forgetting, something important he had to remember. What? He did not know and he almost did not care. But he forced himself to concentrate, while Fever mocked him with the names and faces of some of the many women he had known.

Delilah. Edith. Rose. Their names were a lovely litany. Their faces flickered in the darkness behind his blind eyes.

Magdalena, he thought. Tess. What was it that he should remember? What was it that he must not forget?

The sun! It should be warming the right side of my face as it rode westward through the sky, he thought.

Never mind about the sun, Fever shrieked at him.

My face, my *whole* face, he screamed silently to himself, it's *all* warm. I'm walking right into the sun, so I'm heading west, not south! He had no sooner realized that he was off course when he stumbled again. But he managed to keep his balance and then, arms weakly flailing, he moved on . . .

. . . and felt the ground suddenly give way beneath his boots. He grunted, unable to utter anything more as he felt himself slipping and then sliding and then falling fast down an embankment. His head and shoulders struck the hard-packed earth, as he rolled down toward the rushing water of the Grand River below him, losing his hat in the process.

He hit the water and immediately sank beneath its surface, thinking: Cool, the water's so nice and cool . . . so soothing.

He coughed. Choked. Coughed again. And then, as he tried to breathe and couldn't because of his waterlogged lungs, he realized that he was drowning.

4

Cimarron fought his way up out of the water, and when his head broke the surface, he gasped, barely able to breathe. He gulped hungrily as he drew air into his bursting lungs.

He gagged. He felt his gorge rise. Water poured in a small flood from his mouth. He swallowed hard several times and then gulped noisily again, taking more life-giving air into his oxygen-starved lungs.

His arms flailed furiously in the water as he swam, struggling to stay afloat. But his boots had filled with water and were dragging him down. He bent over, reached down, and tried to pull them off, but he could not do so because the river's swift current suddenly overturned him. His body tumbled head over heels as the current had its way with him. He tried hard to fight it but succeeded only in swallowing more water as he was swept downstream.

When he collided with a cluster of partially submerged rocks, he ignored the sharp pain the impact caused, and blindly tried to seize and hold on to them to halt his headlong flight downriver. But their surfaces above the waterline were jagged and covered with slimy algae and he could not get a firm grip on them. He floated past them, and was once again adrift in the river as it rushed mindlessly onward.

He began to shiver uncontrollably. Unable to see, he could not tell in which direction he was headed.

He tried desperately to find something to grab on to, something he could grip that would help to anchor him however briefly, but only the brittle root of a tree that had been uncovered by the river's waters came to his blindly groping hands. It snapped and he was swept away as the river continued its mad journey.

"Over here!"

He was not certain that he had really heard the words, the words that had just been shouted by a woman his blinded eyes could not see. Had there really been a voice? Or had he only imagined it? Had he manufactured it out of a desperate hope for his own survival mixed with a burning desire to escape from the river's deadly wet clutches? Had Fever whispered the words to him?

He began to swim again, fighting the current, toward the spot he believed the voice had come from, hoping that the voice he thought he had heard was real, and not merely a fevered figment of his imagination. His water-logged boots were deadweights on his feet and they seemed determined to drag him down toward the sandy floor of the riverbed. Blood began to drum in his temples. He swam doggedly on, and as he did so, the woman shouted again, calling his name this time.

"This way! Grab the rope!" she shouted.

What rope? Where? And then it struck his shoulder and he seized it desperately and, following the woman's shouted instructions, pulled its loop down over his torso.

His body screamed in agony then as he was hauled out of the water and up onto the bank of the river. But he kept his teeth gritted and his jaws clamped shut, uttering not the slightest sound. He was alive, he told himself. It was enough. It was everything. The pain did not matter.

As he lay there on the riverbank, his fingers spastically clawing into the mud covering the bank, his chest heaving as he breathed in sweet air, the pounding in his temples gradually begin to subside. He did not care that his mangled face was half-buried in the mud of the riverbank. He did not care that he had lost his hat. He cared only that a woman had come out of nowhere and had saved his life.

"Who are you?" he murmured, his voice little more than a faint ghost of its usual richly resonant self.

And then she was kneeling beside him and gently brushing lank strands of wet hair from his face, and he managed to repeat his question.

"Don't you know me, Cimarron? It's Rupa."

For a split second the name meant nothing to him. And then he remembered the gypsy woman he had first met in the Three Forks Area weeks earlier, and who had only recently told his fortune at the Coweta District Fair. "Rupa? It's really you?" He raised a hand, and it hovered weakly in the air above his chest.

"It's really me," Rupa replied, taking his hand in both of hers.

"What—how—"

"I came searching for you," she whispered.

"You came searching for me?" he repeated, his tone incredulous as he squeezed her hands and then brought them close to his face so that his lips could gently brush them. "How come you did, honey?"

"Because . . ." She fell silent. And then, in a softer tone, "Because I sent word to the Tshurara that you were coming to them because of what Mala had done to your lady friend. I wanted to warn them to beware of you and what you might try to do to them."

So that's how Kore knew my name, Cimarron thought.

"When I told Luluvo what I had done, he was very angry with me. He reminded me of when we first met you at Three Forks—you remember that those religious fanatics had threatened to shoot us because they suspected us of stealing some of their chickens?"

"I remember."

"Luluvo reminded me that you had offered that day to help us in any way you could. He said I had done wrong to betray you to the Tshurara. I did it, I told him, because you were a *gajo*, and although the Tshurara are a troublesome tribe, they are at least gypsies, but you are not. I thought I owed it to them to warn them. Then, after talking to Luluvo, I decided to try to overtake you and keep you away from the Tshurara. But I came too late."

"You came just in time, Rupa. If you hadn't've showed up here when you did, I might well be a goner by now." He removed his boots, poured the water from them, and pulled them back on.

"I talked to Kore of the Tshurara at their camp and he told me what he and his men had done to you and that they had then left you unconscious far south of their camp. I went looking for you. First, I found a horse—a black. I thought it might be yours."

"Did the saddle on it have diamond shapes tooled into the leather?"

"Yes."

"That black, I rented it in Pryor Creek."

"When I first saw you, Cimarron, why didn't you wave when I waved to you?"

"You waved to me?"

"Yes."

"Honey, what Kore and his boys did to me—it's left me blind as a bat, along with feeling like I need sewing up in order to keep from spilling my brains and insides out all over the land."

"Blind?"

Rupa's whispered word drifted in the air between her and Cimarron. And then, as a severe fit of shivering seized him, she helped him to sit up, and then sat beside him, her arms wrapped around him as she sought to share with him the warmth of her own body.

"Got a fever," he told her as he gingerly probed the crusty scales on his wounded face. "Must have got dirt in some of these cuts Kore and his boys made in my hide when I fell down before. If I start talking foolish, honey, you just pay me no mind."

"I am so ashamed of what I have done," Rupa murmured.

"Don't be. You tried looking out for the good of your own people. That's a natural thing to do under the circumstances."

"Do you think you can ride?"

"I can try. Why?"

"We will ride together to Locust Grove."

"What for?"

"I will take care of you there until you are better and can take care of yourself once again. It is the time of year when many gypsies gather at Locust Grove for the horse-trading fair that is held there every autumn."

"I know about that fair. Was at it once. You folks planning on doing some trading there this year, are you?"

"Yes. We gypsies rendezvous, those of us who can, at Locust Grove every year. It is an exciting event in our lives. It is for us, as you *gaje* say, a holiday."

As Rupa rambled on enthusiastically about the gathering of gypsies that was about to take place at Locust Grove, Cimarron fiercely willed himself to see and he saw a tall tree—a lodgepole pine, its leaves turning color and beginning to fall . . .

But he knew he was deceiving himself. In reality, he saw no lodgepole pine. He saw only the summoned memory of a pine in his mind's eye.

"This is your rope," Rupa was saying as she slid the lariat over his shoulders and then over his head. "I found it hanging on the saddle horn of your horse."

He heard her rise and move away from him. He wanted to call her back, suddenly afraid that she had changed her mind and had decided to leave him.

But his fear proved groundless. She returned with a blanket, and after helping him to his feet, she wrapped it around him. "Come," she said, and led him away.

"This is your horse," she said a moment later as she placed his left hand on his saddle horn. "Mine is nearby."

He climbed into the saddle and sat there, his boots thrust deep into his stirrups, holding himself rigid as bright red lights flashed in the deep darkness behind his closed eyelids. He tried to ignore them and also the fire burning within his body and mind, the fire of fever that could not be extinguished despite the icy cold waves washing over him at irregular intervals, leaving his hands shaking and his teeth chattering.

"We will go now," said Rupa, now beside him, and they moved out together, Cimarron alternately giddy and then dizzy, and grateful for the strong hand Rupa placed on his left arm to help steady him in the saddle.

They stopped in Pryor Creek on their way to Locust Grove and there Cimarron returned the black he was riding to the boy at the livery stable. He rooted about in his jeans, came up with a dollar, and handed it to the boy. "That's what I promised to turn over to you for taking good care of my horse," he said as he blindly groped for his bay, to which the stableboy had transferred his gear.

"Thanks," said the stableboy, and then, as Cimarron, fighting a terrible weakness that seemed to sap every ounce of energy from his body, climbed clumsily into the saddle, he heard the boy whisper to Rupa, "What happened to him?"

He did not hear Rupa's murmured answer to the question, but he did hear her ask the stableboy in a clear voice if there was a doctor in Pryor Creek.

"No, ma'am," he heard the stableboy reply. "We had us a doctor, but he was a drunk and he got himself killed falling out of his surrey. Folks here have to travel down to Locust Grove to visit the nearest doctor."

"Cimarron," Rupa said, "would you like to stay here in town for a day or two to rest?"

"Nope. I reckon we'd best be setting out to link up with your people. Once we join up with them, then I can rest. Maybe your folks'll let me abide with you for a spell while I see what the doctor in Locust Grove might have to say about my affliction."

They left the livery and headed south together, Rupa singing softly in Romany.

Yov tover, me pori,
Yov kokosh, me cátrá,
Ádá, ádá me kamav!

64

He found the sound of her voice both soothing and reassuring. "What's that song mean in English?" he asked.

"It means . . . Someday I may tell you."

They had not gone far when he felt himself suddenly and rapidly weakening. His left foot slipped from the stirrup. His body tilted to the right. He grabbed the saddle horn with both hands and held tightly to it, but he lost his grip and fell heavily to the ground.

He heard Rupa's shocked cry and tried hard to get to his feet but he couldn't. It was not until Rupa was beside him and helping him that he was able once again to rise and board his bay.

"You'd best tie me into the saddle," he told her. "That's one way to make sure I stay in it."

"Perhaps we should return to Pryor Creek—"

"No. Do like I said, Rupa."

It took her a long time to obey his order, but she finally succeeded in doing so. When they finally moved out, Cimarron's feet were tied tightly into his stirrups and his hands were just as firmly fastened to his saddle horn.

Cimarron was raving by the time they reached the encampment of the Lowara tribe of gypsies north of Locust Grove.

He alternately sang bawdy songs at the top of his voice while sweat poured from his face and body, and angrily accused Rupa, whom he called Lilah, of deserting him and his infant son when they needed her most.

Rupa quickly summoned the elderly Luluvo, who in turn enlisted the aid of several younger men. They untied Cimarron despite his vociferous protests that they were trying to kill him, managing as they did so to nimbly dodge most of the weak blows he aimed at them. Then they carried him to an empty covered wagon and laid him down on a straw-filled tick and covered him with several blankets. Two of the men held him down until at last he fell into a fitful sleep, during which he sometimes mumbled curses and occasionally cried out in an anguished voice.

He drifted in and out of sleep, in and out of wakefulness,

sweating and throwing off his blankets and then begging for more cover because he was freezing. He did not know how much time had passed when he heard voices near him—Rupa's and that of a man he did not know.

"Take this," the man said to him, inserting a glass tube into his mouth. "Suck on it like you were sipping cider," the man ordered.

Cimarron did, his eyes closed, too weak to protest.

When the glass tube was removed from his mouth, he heard the man say in a voice that seemed to come from far away, "Go and buy some ice at the icehouse in town. Pack him in it. The first thing we've got to do is get his fever down. I'll leave some pills. Give him one every four hours. I'll be back in the morning."

"Thank you, Doctor," he heard Rupa say, and then they were both gone and he was alone. No, he was not alone, he realized as he heard the rumbling voices of two men. He wondered what they were doing there. Guarding him? He wanted to ask them if they knew how to play poker. He wanted . . .

He slept. And dreamed of the three-headed dog named Cerberus he had once read about. The dog that guarded the gates of hell. A dog that would let a man enter hell but would prevent him from leaving it. He patted Cerberus on each of the fearsome animal's three growling heads and walked through the entrance to hell above which hung a sign reading in part: *Abandon hope all ye who enter here.*

He burned in the flames of hell. He shrieked and suffered with the other lost souls. But then, the flames began to die down, to burn low, and finally to go out, all of them.

He was cold again. Shivering. He was unable to move a muscle. He opened his eyes and blinked, still blind, and wondered uneasily where he was and why he was so cold.

He heard someone moving about and then . . . silence. A moment later, he heard more movement, and then someone's soft hands were cradling his face and he thought, fondly remembering, Rupa.

"Cimarron." A gentle hand left his right cheek and

66

came to rest on his forehead. "The fever," he heard Rupa say, "it has broken."

He sighed, suddenly realizing that he was reclining in a tin bathtub packed with ice, which had apparently driven the fever from his body. He heard Rupa speak to someone in Romany and then he felt four strong hands—those of the two men he had earlier thought of as his guards? —help him up and out of the tub. The two men helped him lie down on a tick near the tub, and then someone covered his nakedness with a blanket.

Rupa told him to lie still, that she would return in a moment. When she did, she proceeded to remove the blanket and then to bathe him with a sponge she soaked in a basin filled with lukewarm water, singing softly as she ministered to him.

> *Yov tover, me pori,*
> *Yov kokosh, me cátrá,*
> *Ádá, ádá me kamav!*

The next day the doctor returned to the Lowara camp and Cimarron discovered he was a man who spoke with a disconcerting directness.

"There's nothing wrong with your eyes," he told Cimarron after he had examined them. "There is no apparent damage to either of them. Although you have been bruised and badly cut about the face, I can see no direct damage to either eye. Is it possible, son, that you do not want to see?"

"Not want to see?" Cimarron exclaimed. "What the hell . . . Excuse me, Doc, but what kind of damn fool do you take me for? Not want to see? Of course I want to see! So don't talk foolish!"

"The fact remains," said the doctor calmly, "the tissues of both your eyes are intact, so you should be able to see."

"Don't talk to me about 'should,' Doc. There must be something wrong with me if I can't see. Maybe you're just not smart enough or skilled enough to figure out what it is that's gone wrong with my eyesight."

"I'll grant you that, son. But let me tell you a little

67

story. During the war I was in the army. Nasty business that war was, let me tell you."

"You don't have to tell me, Doc. I was in it too."

"I saw a lot of horrors in that war, son. Saw young boys with the peach fuzz still on their cheeks lose legs I sawed off myself. Saw men—married men, some of them—who wouldn't ever be real men again because . . . Well, let's not go into the gory details. There were times when our field hospital was so awash in blood that I struggled to keep on my feet because the ground grew so red and slippery beneath them."

"What are you getting at, Doc?"

"Just this. Sometimes before a battle—before either side had even fired a shot—I saw hale and hearty men suddenly go lame. They couldn't walk. They *could not walk*."

"I can walk, Doc, so—"

"Some men went blind before a battle. They couldn't see, because they were afraid to see. They knew—without really knowing consciously that they knew—deep down in some dark part of their frightened minds, that if they couldn't see, they wouldn't have to fight, so they simply went blind."

"Wait a minute, Doc. Are you saying I can't see because I don't want to see? That I'm some kind of coward? Is that it? If it is—"

"Fear can do terrible things to people," the doctor mused. "Some of the men I've been talking about later regained the ability to walk—or their sight—after the danger was passed, after the battle was over and they had been transferred to a safe position behind the lines. Some remained permanently crippled."

"Dammit, Doc, I want to see! I'm not playing any kind of games here! My eyes have somehow gone and given out on me! That beating I told you I took—"

"That beating, yes. I'm sure I could not have survived such an awful experience."

"It was pretty bad," Cimarron admitted in a low voice. "If there'd been less of them than there was, I might of held my own against them. But they were a whole big bunch." In his mind's bright eye, Cimarron once again saw the rawhide hondas rising and falling, felt them strike his body, felt the pain they sired in his flesh and in his bones, and he squeezed shut his unseeing eyes, as if by doing so he could banish the ugly vision of what had happened to him.

"I'll come back tomorrow," the doctor said. "Meanwhile, you use that salve I left with Rupa. It's a healer, though it'll take some time for you to fully mend. Stay off your feet as much as possible. Eat good to get back your strength and build up new blood to make up for all that you lost. At the first sign of fever, you send someone to fetch me, hear?"

"Thanks, Doc." Cimarron held out his hand and felt the doctor take and shake it.

"I'm sorry my words got tangled up before," the doctor said. "I can set broken bones and sew up wounds, but I don't always know how to line up words so that they make good sense. Looking at you, son, it's easy to see, from the way you bear up under pain, that there's not a cowardly bone in your body."

When the doctor had gone, Cimarron lay back on his tick, his hands clasped behind his head, and thought about what the doctor said. Men going blind, he thought, on account of they were afraid to fight in the war. Or winding up not able to walk for the same reason. None of it made any sense to him. He wondered if the doctor was trying to cover up his ignorance by telling such unbelievable stories. He wondered if the man was a quack.

The following morning, the elderly Luluvo came to Cimarron's wagon, bringing with him a plate of corn fritters and baked beans. "It is strange, is it not," he remarked as he sat down in the wagon and gave the plate of food he had brought to Cimarron, "how fortune deals with us? You offered to help us when we first met at Three Forks. Now, because of what Kore and his men did to you, we are the ones who are able to help you."

"You know what happened to me up north?"

"Rupa told me that you went to the Tshurara to talk to a woman named Mala. She said that you believe Mala stole some money from a friend of yours and that Kore and his men beat you badly to keep you from seeing her."

"They did that. And that brings up a point, Luluvo. Considering the bad shape I'm in—well, what I'm getting at is I don't want to be a burden to you."

Cimarron felt Luluvo's hand come to rest upon his shoulder. "You are a friend. We Rom do whatever we can to help a friend."

"I've got to find some way to get back to Fort Smith. Maybe you could send out a scout to see if he could round up some other deputy who'd be willing to help me get back to Fort Smith, Luluvo. I know it's a lot to ask and I wouldn't trouble you, except I'm not able to do for myself now that my eyes have given out on me."

"We will do better than that for you," Luluvo volunteered, withdrawing his hand from Cimarron's shoulder. "We are planning to travel east when the horse fair is finished at Locust Grove. We will take you with us and leave you at Fort Smith."

Cimarron stopped eating and stared sightlessly into space. "You're sure that's not out of your way?"

"No place is out of the way for gypsies, Cimarron. We go like the wind—everywhere."

"I'm obliged to you, Luluvo."

"It is settled, then. Now I can speak of the important business that has brought me to you."

"Important business?"

"Tonight we hold *patshiv* and you are invited."

"What's *patshiv?*"

"It is the Rom word for a celebration. For a festival. When you know us gypsies better you will know that we have *patshiv* often . . . at the drop of a hat, as you *gaje* would say. We sing. We dance. We feast. You will come?"

"Sure I'll come, Luluvo. Wouldn't miss it." Cimarron lowered his head.

For a moment, there was a thick silence between the two men. Luluvo, speaking softly, broke it. "You are

70

thinking that you will not be able to see what happens at *patshiv*. It is so, yes?" When Cimarron nodded, Luluvo continued, "You will hear the songs. You can even learn to sing them with us. You will taste the food. You will take the hands of a woman and hold tight to them while the two of you dance."

"I'm having a real hard time getting used to the fact that I can't see, Luluvo."

"I know that. Were I you, I too would mourn the loss of my sight. And yet, you have not lost your life. You live and breathe. Though blind, you can still hear and touch the beauty that is in this old world of ours. You may still make love to a woman. Sire children upon her, if that is your desire. Cimarron, do not, I beg you, let bitterness blossom within you. That would be a very bad thing. We Rom have a saying that applies to a bitter man or woman: *O zalzaro kahl peski piri*. In English, it means, Acid corrodes its own container. Do you take my meaning, Cimarron?"

"I do."

"Good. Now I must go. But I will not leave you alone."

Cimarron looked inquiringly in the direction from which Luluvo's voice had come to him.

"I leave you in the company of a beautiful young woman, Cimarron. Climb into the wagon, Rupa."

"Good morning, Luluvo," Cimarron heard Rupa say, and he found himself damning his blindness that prevented him from seeing her loveliness. "Good morning, Cimarron."

"*Ashen Devlesa*, Cimarron," Luluvo said, and Cimarron felt him take the empty plate from his hand and then climb down from the wagon.

"What did he say?" Cimarron asked Rupa.

"May you remain with God."

"He's a nice old man," Cimarron remarked sincerely. "He's offered to take me with your caravan when you leave here."

"Ah, then you have decided to remain with us on our journey north?"

"North?" The word rang in Cimarron's ear. "Luluvo just told me you folks were heading east. He told me that he'd drop me off in Fort Smith and that you folks would be traveling on from there."

Rupa was silent for a moment. And then, "Luluvo has a heart big enough to hold the whole world within it. He cannot stand by without helping when someone is hurting. He is a good man, and because he is, the Lowara are happy to have him lead them."

"So he's heading east for my sake," Cimarron mused. "You folks had intended to head north."

"That is true."

Cimarron drew a deep breath and then let it out. "You gypsies have your share of homilies and sayings I've learned. Well, us *gaje* have some sayings too, and one of them comes to my mind at the moment. 'A friend in need is a friend indeed.' I want to find Luluvo and tell him about that saying. I'm a man in need and he's held out both of his hands—and the hands of all the people he's leading, too—to help me, and that makes me a mighty grateful man. I want to tell him so. I want to tell him that if I can ever do anything for him—though what a man in my afflicted condition could ever do to help him or you folks I just don't know—I'll be more than eager and willing to do it. Will you lead me to him?"

Rupa took Cimarron's hand and helped him climb down from the wagon.

They found Luluvo chatting with several men at a nearby cooking fire.

"Got something to say to you, Luluvo," Cimarron said, drawing the man aside. When he had expressed his feelings to Luluvo as he had done a moment ago to Rupa, the two men shook hands warmly.

"Would you like to take a walk?" Rupa asked Cimarron when Luluvo had returned to the fire.

"Sure. Lead the way."

She took his hand and led him away from the camp into the growth of pines that bordered it on the north and that served the camp as an effective windbreak. They talked as they walked, Rupa telling Cimarron about the impending celebration, about how excited she was about it, and would he promise to dance with her during it; about the rumors that the Tshurara were sending some of their young men south to the horse-trading fair—

"Those bastards," Cimarron exclaimed, interrupting Rupa. "They're coming here?"

"Some more of the Lowara arrived at our camp this morning. They said that, as they passed the Tshurara camp up north, they met many men making ready to travel here with many horses."

"If that Kore's with them, I'll kill the son of a bitch!" Cimarron muttered under his breath. Then, "I'm sorry to talk so harsh in front of you, Rupa. It's just that—"

She placed an index finger on his lips to silence him. "I understand. But you will not fight Kore or anyone else, should the Tshurara come here. You cannot. It would be foolishness to try to do so, since you cannot see."

He brushed her finger aside. "I don't need to see for what I'm intending to do. All I need to do is get close enough to Kore to get my hands around his throat—"

He heard the woman running away from him, then he called her name.

"I will not listen to you talk of fighting, of killing," she cried out from some distance away. "I do not want you to be hurt again."

"Sounds like you don't have a whole lot of faith in my fighting ability," he called out to her in an attempt to make light of the matter that had so obviously disturbed her. He made his way slowly in the direction from which her voice had come. Conscious of the sun on his bare head as he walked, he brushed aside low-hanging branches, and realized that the stand of trees was thinning out around him. "Rupa? Where are you?"

She did not answer him. But he heard a sound and it was a familiar one.

Whirrrttt.

His hand dropped to his gun and landed on his empty

holster. Gone, he thought. That goddamned Kore's got my six-gun.

Whirrrttt.

He hurried on and then halted, listening. What the hell am I going to do now? he asked himself. I've got no gun, and even if I had one, what good would a gun do a sightless man like me?

"Rupa? Don't move! Is it near you, the sidewinder?"

"Yes!" came Rupa's weak reply. "It's right in front of me. It's going to— Oh, Cimarron, help me!"

He cursed his blindness, cursed a fate that could make him helpless in the face of a rattler about to strike Rupa, and he could see neither her nor the deadly snake that threatened her life.

And then, as his silent curses reached a crescendo in his anguished mind, they seemed to explode in a flurry of gaudy fireworks. And he saw Cerberus guarding the gates of hell, saw Lilah and his infant son standing with a blinding sun behind them, saw the sidewinder, its body tightly coiled and its head and tail raised as it stared coldly at the rigid Rupa, who stood only feet away from it, her back pressed up against the trunk of a loblolly pine . . .

He wanted to shout with joy because suddenly *he could see again!*

But he made no sound. He moved stealthily forward, his eyes boring into the sidewinder. He circled around behind it and moved up on it. When he was directly behind the snake, his knees bent and his right hand shot out, darting toward it. His fingers closed on the rattler's raised and whirring tail. He adroitly jerked the snake upward from the ground and deftly snapped its body as if it had been a whip.

There was a dull popping sound as the maneuver severed the sidewinder's head from its body.

He dropped the snake's squirming body and hurried toward Rupa, who, when she saw him coming, ran into his arms. They stood there, holding tightly to each other, while she sobbed with relief. He brushed away her tears

74

and she looked up at him and uttered a single word: "How?"

"I can see again," he told her exultantly.

Her eyes widened as she stared up at him and then she was hugging him, alternately sobbing and laughing, and he was holding her close to him, knowing at last what people meant when they spoke of miracles.

5

That night, as fireflies and a huge bonfire illuminated the darkness of the night and violins played, Cimarron sat with Luluvo on one side of him and Rupa on the other and declared, "That doctor was right all along, though I'll confess I had started thinking he was a charlatan when he told me maybe I didn't want to see."

"I was petrified," Rupa announced for the second or third time. "I thought surely I would not live to see another day—or even this *patshiv*. But Cimarron saved me from that horrible snake."

"My sight," he mused, "it just came back to me when I needed it, and needed it bad—so I could save Rupa. I guess I lost it the same way. On account of I didn't want to see what the Tshurara were doing to me with those rawhide ropes of theirs. But when the chips were down, when I needed to see, I saw!"

Luluvo dipped his fingers into a bowl of food and stuffed them into his mouth. Then, tapping an index finger against his forehead, he remarked, "The mind of a man is a marvelous thing. It is the means by which his soul may soar and, sadly, it is also the source of his many torments."

Cimarron dipped his fingers into a bowl passed to him by Luluvo and tasted the food it contained. "Good. What is it?"

"Hedgehog," Luluvo told him. "It is seasoned with garlic and black pepper."

Cimarron dipped up more of the delicately textured but slightly gamy and very fat meat and ate it.

"I would like a beer," Luluvo said, and belched loudly. "Would you, Cimarron? Rupa?"

Cimarron nodded as Rupa shook her head, and then she whispered something to him when Luluvo left them to go to the barrel tapped at the camp's far side.

Returning with two huge glasses filled with beer, Luluvo handed one to Cimarron, who drank and then belched loudly several times in succession. Rupa, during Luluvo's absence, had urged him to do so, to show his appreciation of the food and the *patshiv* in general, as was the custom among gypsies.

The three of them sat in silence then, listening to the stirring sounds of the violins and watching the sometimes frantically whirling and spinning dancers. Gaudy colors flashed in the light of the lanterns—the women's kerchiefs and skirts, the men's shirts and vests—orange, yellow, gold, green, violet, fuchsia, amber, blue. Feet stomped the already hard-packed earth. The violins continued to keen. Somewhere in the distance, an unseen dog barked. Children scampered merrily about the area while their younger brothers and sisters sat sleepy-eyed and leaned against their mothers.

Luluvo rose to his feet. He raised his half-empty glass and gave a loud shout. When he had the attention of the other Lowara, he began to sing, softly at first, his voice gradually rising until it seemed to fill the entire night.

"Luluvo sings the *patshivaki djili*," Rupa whispered to Cimarron.

As she spoke, Luluvo turned and solemnly bowed in Cimarron's direction.

"The *patshivaki djili*," Rupa whispered, "is the *patshiv* song—a special song for the occasion. Luluvo sings in praise of the brave deed you did today, Cimarron. Of how you saved my life."

He suddenly became aware of the hush that had fallen

on the gypsies and of the covert and, in some cases, bold and admiring glances that many of the Lowara gave him as Luluvo sang on enthusiastically in the Romany language.

"Luluvo sings that you are a fearless man," Rupa translated. "That you are a man not afraid of anything in the whole wide world—"

Not true, Cimarron thought, but he said nothing.

"—and that the Lowara are fortunate to number such a man among their good friends."

Luluvo's voice dropped. He cast his eyes down as he went on singing.

"He sounds like his favorite dog just died," Cimarron murmured. "What's made him sound so sad all of a sudden?"

"He sings of the time that is coming soon when you, the brave friend of the Lowara, will leave us." Rupa paused and then, without looking directly at Cimarron, asked, "You will leave us now that you have regained your sight?"

"I've got to get back to Fort Smith, Rupa. I've got a job to do, my living to earn."

She nodded mutely.

"Hey, honey, don't look so sad. We'll meet again, you and me. Somewhere. Sometime."

"Maybe we will. Maybe we will not."

Luluvo's voice rose and he was joined in his singing by the other Lowara men, all of whom turned now to face Cimarron. They all bowed ceremoniously in his direction, concluding their song with the solemnly spoken words: *Zhan le Devlesa tai sastimasa.*

"They say, 'Go with God and in good health,' " Rupa told Cimarron.

He stood up then and, following her hurriedly whispered directions as she rose to stand beside him, bowed to the men facing him and uttered the words she had told him to say: "*Ray baro.*"

Smiles wreathed the faces of the Lowara men. They murmured among themselves while turning their eyes upon Cimarron and giving him appreciative glances.

"What did I just say to them?"

" 'Great Lords,' " Rupa answered. "See how pleased

they all are that you returned their compliments with one of your own—and in Romany!"

The violins, which had fallen silent, began again to play and a man in the crowd shouted something in Romany.

"He spoke your name," Cimarron remarked, and Rupa nodded.

"They want me to dance," she told him. "And I shall. But let me tell you a secret first. It is not for the Lowara that I dance, Cimarron. It is for you."

"Well, now, that's real nice of you, honey, to give me a gift like that. It beats any I can remember getting ever before, even come Christmas time. I promise you I'll properly appreciate it with my brand-new eyes, and that's the truth!"

Rupa left his side, spoke briefly to the men with the violins, and then, as they began to play a raucously lilting melody, she began to dance, slowly at first and then much faster.

Her arms were raised above her head and Cimarron noted the way her breasts, so firm and provocative beneath her yellow silk blouse, lifted. He noted, too, the way her several vibrantly colored skirts swirled about her shapely legs as she twirled and turned, first one way and then the other. Her hair, which had become undone, flew around her face as if to mask it, and then slipped away to reveal her features' firelit beauty.

The men watching her began to clap in rhythm with the voices of the violins. Rupa threw back her head, her lips parted, her right leg lifted high off the ground, her skirts a frothy mass about her exposed thigh. She pitched forward, bent almost double, her hair hanging down. She straightened, turned, and boldly faced Cimarron. She held out her hands to him. She beckoned to him. He glanced to one side and the Lowara men shouted encouragement to him. He stepped forward and joined Rupa.

The violins played more softly, more slowly, now. Rupa moved sinuously in front of Cimarron, her torso swaying from one side to the other. He too moved, and as sinuously. They undulated, facing each other like two tall serpents, and then, as if obeying some unheard and unseen signal, both of them began to circle each other. Rupa's hands reached out but did not quite touch Cimarron's chest. His hands reached for her but she eluded his grasp as they continued circling, their hips rocking in a subtle imitation of what was clearly a sexual act, their eyes locked on each other.

Cimarron felt himself stiffening. The woman facing him, the siren luring him to her, was the very essence of desire. The way her body moved, the light that glowed deep in her eyes, everything about Rupa was calculated to arouse—and arouse Cimarron she did, until his long and stone-hard shaft was pressed tightly against his confining jeans.

The world was lost to him then except for the faintly sad song of the violins and Rupa, an incandescent vision of loveliness undulating in front of him like the very embodiment of all that was female and desirable and irresistible—

The gypsy camp suddenly seemed to explode in raucous sound.

The violins died. Men shouted. Women screamed. Rupa stood stricken in front of Cimarron, staring into the ominous night beyond the light of the camp's bonfire.

He turned, still lost in the lusty vision that Rupa had aroused within him, and saw the mounted men riding swiftly out of the trees and into the center of the camp, heard them shouting, saw the guns in their hands.

The leader of the horde drew rein, dismounted, and demanded in a loud and overbearing voice to speak to the man he called "the King of the Gypsies."

"We gypsies have no king," said Luluvo, stepping forward. "But I will speak to you and try to satisfy your desires, sir."

Cimarron stepped forward to stand beside Luluvo.

"Who are you?" barked the man who had just spoken.

"A friend of these folks, for one thing," Cimarron replied. "For another"—he pulled his badge from his pocket—"I'm a deputy marshal out of Fort Smith. Now, why don't you tell me who you happen to be?"

"Captain Varnum, Cherokee Lighthorse," the man snapped.

"What can we do for you, esteemed Captain?" purred Luluvo, rubbing his hands together, his tone ingratiating.

"You can get yourselves the hell out of here," Varnum bellowed. "All of you. We're tired of the trouble you've been making for the citizens of Cherokee Nation and we're not going to put up with any more of it. Your women sow discontent among us with their roadside fortune-telling. Your children thieve from local merchants. Your men make our young men fight them because of the way they treat our young women."

"You must have us mistaken with some other kind of gypsies," Luluvo offered. "The notorious Tshurara, for example. We are peaceful people, esteemed Captain. Law-abiding people. We—"

"Have you got any proof of the charges you're leveling, Varnum?" Cimarron interrupted.

"Pack up and move out," Varnum ordered, ignoring Cimarron's question. "Be gone from here before morning, or I will not be responsible for what may happen to you."

"What do you reckon might happen?" Cimarron asked, his eyes narrowing.

"The Cherokees are up in arms and hot under the collar," Varnum told him. "We've put up with enough— more than enough—from these damned gypsies. We'll put up with no more. I've given you fair warning. If the hotbloods among my people decide to do more than just talk troublemaking, if they decide to maybe bring back the old days when scalp-taking was in fashion—well, I've just told you that I'll not be responsible for what happens."

"You say you've got no proof that these folks have committed any kind of crime," Cimarron pointed out. "Then it seems to me you've got no right to try to run them off. Maybe we could work out some kind of arrangement, me and you, Captain." Cimarron beckoned and Varnum left his men and followed Cimarron to the far side of the bonfire.

"What kind of arrangement are you talking about?" Varnum asked him skeptically when he had halted.

Cimarron summoned Luluvo before answering the question. Then, after speaking briefly to Luluvo, he turned back to Varnum. "What would you, as the duly constituted authority here in Cherokee Nation, say to a proposal my friend Luluvo here's just come up with?"

"What kind of proposal?"

"Luluvo proposes to post bond—in gold—to reassure you Lighthorsemen and the good citizens of Cherokee Nation that they mean no harm to any of you or to your property. If these gypsies don't live up to their end of the bargain, why, you can just confiscate the bond they've posted with you and run them off as disturbers of the peace—or worse, depending on whatever kind of crime they might commit in the future. If, though, they hold up their end of the bargain and make no trouble, then you'll hand them back their gold when they're ready to pull up stakes and leave here."

"How much gold are you prepared to put up as bond?" Varnum asked.

Luluvo answered, "One hundred dollars."

"Two hundred," Varnum countered.

Luluvo shrugged, turned away, and moved through the crowd of silent gypsies. When he returned nearly half an hour later, he was carrying a gunnysack full of gold pieces and a paper. He handed both to Varnum and said, "There are two hundred dollars in the sack. Please sign the paper to indicate that you have received our bond, which has been given to you in good faith on behalf of the Lowara."

Varnum first counted the money in the gunnysack and only then, using a stubby pencil Luluvo handed him, did he sign the receipt for the gold and hand it back to Luluvo.

"You satisfied now, Varnum?" Cimarron asked him.

"I still think your friends would be wiser to move out of the area," Varnum responded coldly. "I told you that there are those of us among the Cherokees who are not unwilling to deal with our enemies as we once did years ago in our many bloody battles back East."

"I hope your hotblooded friends don't take any such

nasty notions into their heads," Cimarron remarked mildly. "If they do, they'll have me to reckon with."

"You have no jurisdiction in this matter," Varnum shot back. "You have jurisdiction over whites—and over Indians only when white people are injured because of a crime committed by an Indian. These people"—Varnum gave a deprecating wave of his hand, a dismissive gesture—"are not white nor are they Indians." He spat. "It is hard to tell how one should categorize them—perhaps as mongrels."

"Jurisdiction be damned!" Cimarron spat. "I'm fed all the way up to here with you and your haughty ways, Varnum. So just let me state one more time—and you make sure you hear what I'm saying to you—if you come around harassing these folks, you come prepared to try the same trick on me. But if you do, I have to give you fair and full warning. I can be mean when an officious bastard such as yourself starts bragging to me about what I can and can't do. I'd say you ought to take that two hundred dollars in gold you're packing, and take your boys and ride the hell out of here. Right now. *And fast!*"

Varnum was about to speak but he apparently thought better of it. Giving Cimarron a sullen look, he wheeled his horse, circled the bonfire, rejoined his men waiting in the distance, and rode away with them.

"Perhaps now we shall have peace," Luluvo said with a sigh as he watched the Lighthorsemen ride into the woods. "But did you hear, Cimarron? Did you hear the esteemed captain's talk of Indian scalp-hunters?" Luluvo's hand rose and nervously covered the crown of his head.

Cimarron, thoughtfully stroking his chin, was silent for a moment and then, without answering Luluvo's question, said, "I was told by Rupa that you folks are here at Locust Grove to attend the annual horse-trading fair. It strikes me that I ought to stop by the fair and see if maybe I can trade my bay for a better mount. Or maybe buy me a good saddle horse and use my bay—he's getting on in years—as a pack animal. When are you all going to the fair, Luluvo?"

"We go in the morning. We have many horses to trade. I am glad you will come with us. I was sad to think of you leaving the Lowara, Cimarron."

"Then I'll attend the fair with you if that's all right."

Luluvo promised to meet Cimarron at the rope corral west of the Lowaras' camp early the following morning, and when the man had left him, Cimarron stood his ground in the firelit darkness thinking of what Capt. Varnum had said earlier. Not said, he thought, so much as threatened. Him and his talk of scalping. His thoughts roamed back over the stories he had heard from various sources in the last several years during the time he had spent as a deputy marshal in Indian Territory. The stories he had heard about the five civilized tribes and their far-from-civilized history. The stories about the Cherokees' and other Indians' early days in the eastern United States before their forced removal to the Territory by the United States government.

They had all been warriors then, he had learned, and bloodthirsty ones. They had easily ranked as bloodthirsty as any of the Plains Indians and they were as adept at torture, rapine, pillage, and murder as any Apache, Sioux, or Comanche had ever been.

His eyes roved among the Lowara as they quietly dispersed, the music of their violins lost, their voices hushed now as a result of their uneasy encounter with the *gajo* law—the Cherokee Lighthorsemen. He caught a glimpse of Rupa just before she disappeared in the crowd. He gritted his teeth as a vision of her, a bloody expanse of hairless flesh where her scalp had been, darted through his mind. He turned away, wondering if Luluvo had believed him when he claimed that he had suddenly decided to delay his departure because he wanted to attend the horse-trading fair at Locust Grove.

He didn't know, and he decided that it really didn't matter what Luluvo believed. What did matter was that he had decided to stay with the Lowara awhile longer. Why? He couldn't give himself a single answer to his question. There were, he had realized earlier, several reasons why he didn't want to leave the Lowara just yet. Rupa was one of those reasons. He didn't want to leave her. Not yet, not before he had a chance to—he smiled— get to know her a bit better. And he was determined to have another try at getting back the money the Tshurara gypsy woman Mala had stolen from Serena Farthing. And he itched to settle his score with Kore of the Tshurara tribe. If those reasons, singly or collectively, were not enough, he had one more, one solidly compelling reason for remaining with the Lowara awhile longer: he wanted to be on hand in case any war-whooping Cherokees gone back to the blanket came bursting into the Lowara camp some night with scalping knives in their hands and blood lust in their eyes.

Cimarron was almost asleep in the covered wagon he had occupied since arriving at the Lowara camp when he heard a stealthy sound in the night outside. He sat up, seized his Winchester, which he had placed beside him, and listened intently. The sound came again. Soft footfalls. Then the canvas cover was drawn aside and moonlight eased into the wagon.

"Hold it right there," he muttered, his finger pressing tensely against the trigger of his rifle. "Who are you and what are you after?"

"It's me, Cimarron."

"Rupa?"

She climbed into the wagon and closed the canvas cover behind her.

He heard her groping her way toward him on her hands and knees, and then she took the rifle from his hands, laid it down, and sat down beside him, her right arm encircling his naked body.

"What are you doing here, honey?" he asked her, drawing her closer to him, hoping he knew the answer to his question.

"I want to be with you," she replied. "I've wanted that for a long time. Almost since the first time I saw you, when you came to my tent at the Coweta District Fair to have your fortune told."

"You didn't tell me then," he whispered in her ear as he nuzzled it, "that I'd have the good fortune to get a visit from you in the middle of the night like this."

"You must think me bold and shameless, coming here like this."

"I think you're a lovely lady and I'm glad you came to keep me company." His right hand roved over her flannel nightdress and then under it, causing Rupa to moan and arch her back.

She moaned again as his hand cupped her hot mound and then began to gently finger her while outside, in the otherwise-silent night, a coyote yipped as if in response to Rupa's low moans.

Cimarron eased her down on her back on his tick and then lay down beside her. She sat up. "Honey, what—" And then he realized what she was doing. She was slipping her nightdress over her head and casting it aside. She lay down beside him again and embraced him, her lips finding his, her tongue working its way past his lips and into the hot cavern of his mouth.

He fondled her breasts, teased her nipples into erect life, thrust his tongue into her mouth. As he eased over upon her, she shifted position beneath him, adroitly adjusting her body to his.

We fit like a key in a lock, he thought as he eased his stiff shaft into the moist warmth of her body. His skin prickled as he plunged deeper into her. His scalp tingled. And then, as she responded to him by thrusting upward and tightly wrapping both of her arms around him, he felt his toes begin to curl.

He pressed down upon her, flattening her breasts beneath him, his bucking increasing in its intensity. His breath began to come in short shallow gasps and the lusty sounds he was making blended with the sighs and occasional grunts of pleasure that escaped Rupa's parted lips.

He felt her fingernails bite into his back and then, as her hands seized his buttocks and she plunged upward against him and cried out, her body convulsing, he too reached the erotic crescendo orchestrated by the wild and sensuous movements of her body so hotly pressed against his own.

He was vaguely aware of the coyote yipping in the distance, and he too wanted to yip, to howl his pleasure into the night as he flooded Rupa and she, writhing with pleasure, heaved and held him close to her as if she never intended to release him.

Then, as their bodies gradually became still and their breathing slowed, Cimarron, the left side of his face pressed against Rupa's cheek, heard her begin to sing softly as she gently ran her fingers through his hair.

> "Yov tover, me pori,
> Yov kokosh, me cátrá,
> Ádá, ádá me kamav!"

"You sang that song before," he murmured, remembering as he lay sated and spent beside Rupa. "Only you wouldn't tell me what it meant."

"Now I will tell you what it means," she whispered, and playfully nipped his earlobe. "He the ax, I the helve. He the cock, I the hen. This, this I will!"

Cimarron raised himself on one elbow and caressed Rupa's cheek. "That's some song, that is."

"There is more to it. It goes like this. 'Many earths on earth there be. Whom I love my own shall be. Grow, grow willow tree! Sorrow none unto me!' And then comes the part I just translated for you. Gypsy women sing that song to bewitch the man they desire. But I think you will not be bewitched by my song because I did not, as custom demands, find your footprint, dig out the earth within its outline, and bury that earth beneath a willow tree while singing the witching song."

"Honey, you don't need any songs to bewitch me. You're beautiful enough to bewitch a man like me without ever even opening your mouth to sing any witching song."

"Do you think I'm pretty, then?"

"Nope."

"You don't?"

"Not pretty. Beautiful's what I said you are."

Rupa seized him, pulled him down upon her, and kissed him passionately.

This time, when the coyote yipped, Cimarron did not hear it because his mind was on what he was doing and what he was doing to Rupa brought him such pleasure that he could think of nothing else.

When Cimarron awoke the next morning, he was alone in the wagon. He got up, dressed, and then joined the other men at a nearby stream. He washed in the icy water before making his way back to the Lowara camp, which was breaking up. As many of the gypsies moved their wagons out, the young Lowara boys, as was their custom, ran beside the wagons so as not to tire the horses.

He spotted Rupa hunkered down beside a campfire and he approached her, a smile on his face. She looked up as he arrived at her fire and offered him a bowl of gruel. He took it from her and spooned some of the hot substance into his mouth. "I missed you this morning," he told her.

She put a finger to her lips and looked around uneasily. "Gypsy women are not supposed to do what I did last night," she said in a low voice. "I left the wagon before dawn so that no one would see me leave it."

"I'm mighty glad the two of us got together last night."

Rupa offered him a cup of coffee, which he accepted. "Looks like most of your people are heading for the Locust Grove fairgrounds," he observed. "Are you fixing to attend the trading?"

"Yes."

"Good. Maybe we'll see each other there."

"You'd better go if you've finished the gruel and coffee," she advised him. "If people see us too much together, tongues will wag."

"Well, honey, I sure don't want to make any move that'll sully your reputation." He handed his empty cup and bowl to Rupa. "I'm obliged to you for the breakfast."

He made his way to the camp corral, where he found

Luluvo waiting for him. He greeted the old man and then, noticing the frown on Luluvo's face, asked, "Something bothering you?"

"Some of the men and women of the Tshurara tribe came to our camp last night," Luluvo replied. "They say their camp north of here has been troubled by Cherokee mischief-makers who stole two of their horses and burned one of their wagons. Fortunately, no one was hurt."

"You don't look happy about having the Tshurara here."

"I am not. That is a sad truth, but a truth nonetheless. One should not turn a stony face toward one's own people. But wherever the Tshurara go, they stir up trouble. And after the visit we received last night from Captain Varnum of the Cherokee Lighthorse, I confess that I wish the Tshurara would go away, far away from the Lowara. Those gypsies bring trouble with them the way a spring wind brings rain."

Cimarron was about to say more when Luluvo somewhat impatiently hailed a young man who was inside the corral, trying his best to get one of the horses to show some spirit. "Bring me a bucket, Yayal," Luluvo ordered the young man.

Yayal left the corral and returned a moment later carrying a tin pail, which he handed to Luluvo.

"I will need some stones, Yayal," Luluvo declared, his eyes scanning the ground. Moments later, after Yayal had gathered the pebbles, Luluvo instructed him to drop them into the pail.

"Bring your stallion," Luluvo ordered Yayal, and then he strode away from the corral, followed by Cimarron.

When they were some distance away from it, and Yayal had joined them with his horse, Luluvo said, "I will show you both how we gypsies put right, as we say, a horse that may not be the best example of its kind in the world. This one obviously lacks spirit. It is old and tired. Like me. But never mind about me. We shall try to change that so that one of the *gaje* will be happy to take this poor dejected nag off Yayal's hands." Luluvo proceeded to vigorously rattle the pebbles in his pail under the horse's nose, causing the animal to shy away.

He rattled them again, even louder this time, and the horse, frightened, reared and tried to break free of Yayal. Luluvo walked around the horse and again rattled the pebbles, making a terrible racket this time. The horse circled, dragging Yayal with it, its eyes wide as it pranced nervously about.

Luluvo spoke briefly to Yayal and then handed him the pail. "Come, Cimarron, let us go the fair."

Later that morning, the two men rode onto the Locust Grove fairgrounds. They dismounted and tethered their horses to a shin oak, then made their way to where count-less horses stood tied to long ropes suspended between wooden poles. Buyers and sellers moved among them, arguing vociferously and slapping one another's hands as first a price was set and then a counteroffer presented.

Through the crowd wandered an old man selling buggy whips and quirts. An old woman sat on the seat of a wagon and loudly hawked wares piled in the bed behind her—worn and obviously secondhand harness, bridles, horse blankets, saddles, and currycombs.

Another gypsy hailed Luluvo, and Cimarron stood by as the two men discussed the horses the newcomer hoped to sell. Cimarron, listening, learned from the trader that the man had "bled the beasts, purged them, and even wormed one or two so that the *gaje* will think I have the equivalent of Arabian steeds to sell today, although the good Lord well knows that half my mounts may be halt or blind or even dead within a fortnight while I, rascal that I am, will be gloating over the profit I have made on them because I bought them cheap and sold them dear."

Cimarron excused himself and rode into Locust Grove, where he stopped at a dry-goods store and bought himself a new black slouch hat with a rawhide band to replace the one he had lost in his battle with Kore and the other Tshurara gypsies. He shaped it until he was satisfied, then clapped the low-crowned and curled-brim hat on his head, paid the store clerk, and returned to the fairgrounds.

He had no sooner rejoined Luluvo, who was alone now, than the old man surprised him by snatching the hat from his head and ripping its sweat band.

"*Te khalion tai te shingerdjon tshe gada, hai tu te trais sastimasa tai voyasa,*" Luluvo stated, and then handed the damaged hat back to Cimarron.

"What the hell did you go and do that for?" Cimarron bellowed testily. "I just bought this here hat for ten dollars and fifty cents and now, thanks to you, it looks like it's been through at least one of the Seventh Cav's campaigns!"

"Let me say what I just said in your language, Cimarron. May your clothes rip and wear out, but may you live on in good health and in fulfillment. It's an old gypsy custom. A way of wishing well to one's friends."

Cimarron nodded somewhat sheepishly, ashamed now of his angry outburst, and clapped his new hat back on his head. A familiar voice interrupted his apologies to Luluvo.

"A fine horse! Fit for a prince—indeed, a king—to ride, good sir! See what a fine top line he has! Look you at his strong teeth!"

Cimarron and Luluvo both turned at the sound of the man's voice to find Yayal displaying his weary nag to a *gajo* who was eyeing the animal skeptically.

"Now, if Yayal will but follow my advice," Luluvo murmured as if he were talking to himself. And then, beaming, he seized Cimarron's arm and pointed at the small boy standing not far away with Yayal's tin pail in his hands. "Watch!" he commanded, and Cimarron watched as Yayal continued to try to convince the *gajo* to buy the next-to-worthless horse he was offering for sale.

"The boy—he is Yayal's younger brother," Luluvo explained. Cimarron saw Yayal gesture behind the *gajo's* back, and then watched as his brother began to rattle the pail, which was still partially filled with pebbles.

At the raucous sound, Yayal's horse began to prance. It shook its head as it high-stepped and circled Yayal and the *gajo*, who nodded appreciatively.

Luluvo laughed as Yayal's younger brother held the pail high above his head so that the horse could see it.

The horse continued to move nervously about while Yayal extravagantly praised the animal's spirit. Moments later, after a spirited exchange, the sale was completed and the *gajo* proudly led his prize away.

Grinning from ear to ear and counting the folding money in his hand, Yayal joined Cimarron and Luluvo. He thanked the older man for his advice on making his horse seem so full of life when it was, in reality, Yayal merrily admitted, placid and perhaps dull-witted.

"But, by the time that *gajo* discovers the sad truth, we will all be far away from here," Luluvo declared solemnly, and then he too began to grin.

"That sure was some shrewd trick," Cimarron told the two men. "I've seen some sharp horse-traders in my time—men who could sell you a half-dead horse they'd made look like he was ready and willing to run a five-mile race. But what you boys just did, it sure beats all I've ever seen where sly horse-trading's concerned."

"We gypsies have many secrets when it comes to horse-trading," Luluvo declared as Yayal left to join his younger brother. "To make an old horse's wind strong for a short time, we feed the beast hen's bane mixed with elderberries. To—"

A disturbance nearby interrupted whatever Luluvo had been about to say. As both men turned toward the sound of shouting, Cimarron muttered, "There's Kore, the son of a bitch! See him in the middle of that mob over there?"

"Ah, so it is," Luluvo said sadly. "I wish I were a wizard and could cast a spell that would make him and those Tshurara men with him vanish into thin air, never to be seen again, any of them."

But Cimarron hadn't heard Luluvo because the old gypsy was hurrying toward Kore, who was arguing volubly with several *gaje*, while other male members of the Tshurara tribe stood stolidly beside him.

When he reached the group, Cimarron was about to speak to Kore when one of the *gaje* accosted him. "Mister, do me a favor and take a look at that horse this wily son just sold me! He cheated me! My friend here checked the horse right after I bought it, and he says it looks to him like somebody's gone and bored holes in the nag's teeth and stuffed them full of some kind of herb to make him seem a whole lot younger than he really is. My friend thinks these goddamned gypsies went and put rosemary in the holes they bored in this sorry critter's teeth."

"I don't know anything about that," Cimarron told the man, his eyes on Kore.

But the buyer of Kore's horse would not be denied. He begged Cimarron to examine the horse.

While Kore glared at him, Cimarron relented and carefully examined the horse in question. When he had done so, he pronounced the animal an old-timer. "He's twelve, probably closer to fifteen years old. Take a look at the way his teeth are all ground down from grazing. He's not worth the powder to blow him up."

"I want my money back," the horse-buyer roared at Kore. "You cheated me and I got this man as a witness to prove you did! Now, you hand me back my money and I'll hand you back your horse and we'll call the matter quits."

Kore turned his back on the man and started to walk away. He didn't get far.

Cimarron reached out, grabbed his shoulder, and spun him around. "You heard the man," he told Kore. "Give him back his money and take back your horse."

"I warned you," Kore shot at Cimarron, "to leave the Tshurara alone. I told you that if you didn't, you'd live to regret it."

"And another thing, while you're making amends," Cimarron added, ignoring Kore's threat, "that there's my forty-four you got stuck in your waistband and I want it back." He didn't wait for Kore to hand him the gun. He jerked it from Kore's waistband and holstered it.

Kore, his eyes wild, spluttered words that Cimarron could not understand and then his right fist flew in front of him.

His haymaker took Cimarron on the chin, sending him staggering backward. He straightened, shook his head to clear it, and went for Kore, fire in his eyes and murder in his heart.

6

Kore moved to one side to avoid the oncoming Cimarron,
but Cimarron merely swerved and continued moving in
on Kore.

Kore threw a wild right jab that glanced off Cimarron's
shoulder, following it up with a left hook that landed on
Cimarron's jaw. Undeterred, Cimarron swung a round-
house right that seemed to lift Kore off the ground when it
smashed into his face, and blood began to flow from Kore's
nose. Cimarron walked into the man with a series of
punishing body blows that landed, one after the other, in
Kore's soft midsection and against his ribs.

Kore was breathing heavily now, the streaming blood
from his nose staining his lips and teeth. He circled Cimarron, watching for an opening, his fists raised but his
head sagging so that his chin was almost touching his
chest.

Cimarron gave him no opening, only a swift and steady
hammering with both fists that sent Kore crashing to the
ground.

A yell went up from the men watching the fight, and
then, out of the corner of his eye, Cimarron saw several of
the Tshurara begin to move in on him. He turned,
unleathered his .44, and barked, "Hoist them and stand
hitched!"

The gypsies halted. They raised their hands.

"I'll take that gun if it's all right with you," Luluvo said, stepping up beside Cimarron. "I'll hold off these dogs while you finish your business with Kore."

"Much obliged." Cimarron turned back to Kore as Luluvo, with Cimarron's gun in his hand, held the rest of the Tshurara at bay.

Kore got groggily to his feet. He stood not far away from Cimarron, swaying slightly, as he wiped the blood from his lips and chin with the back of one hand. Suddenly, he lunged at Cimarron, his right fist swinging out to slam into Cimarron's chest, his left hand, held rigid with all five fingers together, chopped savagely at Cimarron's throat.

Cimarron managed to deflect the force of Kore's body blow by turning slightly, but the sharp chop caused him to gag and fight mightily to draw air down his burning throat and into his lungs. When Cimarron's guard was down, Kore closed in and used both his fists and his feet to pound the lawman. Cimarron staggered backward under the succession of blows, several of which struck him below the belt. His shins screamed in pain as Kore kicked him twice in rapid succession. He lost his balance and went down.

Kore threw himself on top of him and the two men grappled together while they rolled over and over in the dust. Kore's hands encircled Cimarron's throat and the Tshurara began to squeeze. Cimarron, his back pressed against the ground and with Kore astride him, tore at his opponent's fingers, but he was unable to break their iron grip. Beginning to gag, Cimarron rolled to the left and threw Kore to the ground. For just an instant Kore's grip on Cimarron's throat relaxed. It was long enough. Cimarron ripped Kore's fingers from his throat and, regaining his feet, bent down and hauled the gypsy to his feet. He drew back his right arm and sent his fist flying into Kore's face. The man blinked stupidly, his eyes beginning to glaze. But then, recovering, he brought one knee up like a hammer of bone and viciously rammed it into Cimarron's groin.

Cimarron grunted in pain as he doubled over and clutched his genitals. Kore slammed a hard fist down on the back of the lawman's skull, knocking him to his knees. The gypsy raised his other fist high in the air, but before he could bring it down, a woman in the crowd cried out.

"Rom!" she cried. *"Bolde tut, kako!"*

Kore's fist was about to come crashing down, but Cimarron, anticipating the blow, lurched to one side and it landed harmlessly on his left bicep. He thrust a fist into Kore's gut and then fought his way back to his feet.

"Kore!" the woman screamed.

Kore turned away from Cimarron. His eyes widened. Cimarron, seeing the shocked look on the man's face, wiped the sweat from his eyes and turned to look in the direction in which Kore was staring. His eyes widened in disbelief as he saw Rupa standing not far away. She had raised her several skirts and was wearing nothing beneath them. She boldly displayed herself to Kore, a stony expression on her face as she did so.

"No!" Kore muttered. And again, *"No!"* He began to back away from Cimarron, who became aware that Luluvo and the other gypsy men, Lowara and Tshurara alike, were standing with their backs turned to Rupa so that they could not see what she was doing.

"Marhimé!" Rupa suddenly screeched, pointing an accusing finger at the rapidly retreating Kore. And then, with a look of triumph on her face, she lowered her skirts and smoothed them with ladylike gestures. "It is over," she loudly announced, and Luluvo and the other gypsies turned toward her. "Kore is now unclean and is banished from among us as a result of what I did."

Luluvo went up to Rupa and patted her shoulder.

Cimarron walked slowly and somewhat unsteadily toward the pair, and when he reached them, he asked, "What was that all about?"

It was Luluvo who answered him. "Gypsies consider their women unclean from the waist down. There are rules—strict rules—governing the behavior of women. Women must not, for example, pass in front of a man or

97

between two men but behind them, and if this is not possible, she must say, *'Bolde tut, kako'* which in English means, 'Please turn away.' She must not let her skirts touch a man who is not her own, nor let her garments touch plates, cups, or drinking glasses. If she does, those things become *marhimé*—unclean—and must be destroyed so that they may not soil the next male who uses them.

"What Rupa did just now is to make Kore *marhimé* —unclean. Now no decent gypsy, not even his closest male relatives, will have anything to do with him until the *kris*—the gypsy court—convenes and lifts his burden of uncleanness from him."

"I did it for you, Cimarron," Rupa said softly, her eyes cast down. "I was afraid he would hurt you."

"I'm beholden to you, honey."

"Get him, boys!" yelled the man who had earlier bought the aged horse from Kore. "Don't let him get away with my money!"

Luluvo smiled as the horse buyer and several friends went racing away after the still-retreating Kore, who had turned and fled from them into the nearby woods. Luluvo gave Cimarron's six-gun back to him and remarked, "Let us hope that Kore is a fast and smooth talker, for we Rom say that with good words you can even sell a bad horse."

Cimarron matched Luluvo's grin.

Then, as the crowd that had gathered to watch the fight between Cimarron and Kore began to disperse, Luluvo moved away with them to inspect the horses that were being offered for sale.

When he had gone, Rupa moved closer to Cimarron. "Did you know that Mala is here?"

"She is? Here at the fairgrounds you mean?"

"She came to the Lowara Camp with Kore because of the trouble the Tshurara were having with the Cherokees in their camp in the north."

"Where is she exactly?"

"If I tell you, you will go to her. You will abandon me."

Cimarron reached out and cupped Rupa's chin in his right hand. He raised her head until she was staring into

98

his eyes. "I'm not about to abandon anybody, Rupa. Least of all not somebody as lovely as you. But I've got to go see Mala and try to get my friend's money back from her."

"Mala will not give you back the money she took from your friend. But she will try to take you from me."

She's a possessive little lady, this Rupa, Cimarron thought. She seems to think she's got me when all she's really got is what she can see and touch just so long as it—I—don't disappear on her. "Tell me where Mala is, honey," he prodded. "Don't make me go hunting for her. I've not got even the slightest notion of what she looks like, so were I to have to track her down, why, I'd be gone from you for one good long time, I'll wager. But if you point me out the way to her, I'll be back by your side quicker'n a horse's tail can catch cockleburs."

"She has a tent down there." Rupa pointed beyond the long lines of tethered horses. "She tells fortunes there."

"I'll be back soon as I can." Cimarron kissed Rupa lightly on her cheek and then made his way between two restless rows of horses, turning once to wave to her where she stood with a forlorn expression on her face, watching his departure.

When he spotted the tent that stood by itself on the far side of the fairgrounds, he made his way to it, keenly aware that his Colt was once again in his hip holster and pleased at the feeling of security the gun gave him.

He was about to enter the tent when a bespectacled matron emerged from it, a sewn-up handkerchief clutched tightly in both hands.

"Three days," the woman murmured, sweat glistening on her forehead and upper lip. She stood between Cimarron and the tent entrance, repeating the two words. Then, as if memorizing a difficult lesson, she murmured, "I must not look in the handkerchief for three days. If I look, the spell will be broken. The money will be gone because of the curse on it. I must not—three days—the curse . . ."

Cimarron touched the brim of his hat to the woman, but she remained oblivious to his gesture. He stepped around

99

her and, sure now that he had come to the right place, ducked down and entered the tent.

"Come in, sir," said the strikingly beautiful woman seated at a small round table in the center of the tent on which rested a crystal ball. "Sit down." She indicated a chair on the opposite side of the table, and Cimarron seated himself in it. "What is it you want Mala to do for you?"

Cimarron, staring at Mala's lush body, her big breasts bulging above her low-cut green blouse, thought of an answer to her question, but it was one he did not dare give her. "I'd like to know what the future holds for me," he said instead. "Can you tell me that, Mala?"

"I can."

And, he thought, I can tell you with a fair degree of certainty what the future holds for you, too. Jail, maybe, if you don't cooperate with me. But first, let's see if you'll try to trick me same as you did Serena Farthing back in Muskogee and that lady who just left here.

"Give me your hand and one dollar."

Cimarron paid her the dollar and then held out his hand. Mala took it, turned it over, and stared down at his palm. He listened then as she talked glibly and at length of love and good fortune, both of which were coming his way, she assured him, and of a long journey he would soon take.

"I could read the crystal for you," Mala suggested. "It tells much more, and tells it clearly."

"For how much?"

"Five dollars."

Cimarron dug down into his pocket a second time and came up again with his roll of folding money from which he peeled a five-dollar bill as he had earlier peeled a single. He handed the money to Mala, who tucked it out of sight between her breasts before turning her attention to the crystal. She ran her slender fingers over its smooth surface, frowned, looked up at Cimarron, and then back down at the crystal.

"It remains dark," she said. "That is strange. Something

100

must have come between our spirits so that the crystal cannot reflect your future."

"Then maybe you'd best give me back my money."

Ignoring Cimarron's suggestion, Mala rose and rounded the table. She took his hands in hers and he got to his feet. They stood facing each other for a moment and then she said, "Come closer to me."

Cimarron gladly obeyed her order, and as he stood with her breasts pressed against him, his pelvis against hers, she said, "I can feel our spirits touching. It is good."

What's touching, he thought, sure as hell's not our spirits. Not by a long shot. There's other names, some of them nasty, for the parts of you and me that's touching.

Mala's arms went around him. She drew him even closer to her so that he could feel the heat of her body against his own. Her fingers dug into his back. One of her long legs eased between his.

He sighed with pleasure and closed his eyes, enjoying himself. He waited, suspecting what was about to happen. When it did, without opening his eyes, he seized her hand, which had started to ease into the pocket of his jeans where he kept his money. He held her hand firmly and said, "You're a slick little minx, Mala, but I'm slicker."

She stiffened and tried to pull away from him, but he continued holding tightly to her hand and then, encircling her waist with his free arm, he held her close to him. "You wanted to cozy up to me so's you could get your hands on my poke," he told her, feeling her breath moist against his cheek. "It wasn't on account of our spirits weren't close enough to let you read the big round piece of glass sitting there in the middle of your table."

"Let go of me!"

"I'd been expecting something of the sort from you, Mala, on account of the way you treated a friend of mine down in Muskogee. You remember a lady named Serena Farthing?"

"No!" Mala jerked her arm, trying to free it, but Cimarron's grip remained firm.

"Well, Serena remembers you. In fact, she's not likely

to forget you and the way you cheated her out of her eighty-seven dollars with that handkerchief trick of yours."

Mala suddenly went limp. Her eyes closed as she leaned weakly against Cimarron.

"Go ahead and faint if you have to," he told her coldly. "I'll still be here when you wake up, and if you don't decide to turn over to me the eighty-seven dollars you stole from Miss Farthing, you and me are going to take a little trip together."

Mala made a sudden and, Cimarron thought, truly miraculous recovery. She straightened and gazed boldly into his eyes. "A trip. To where?"

"To the women's jail in Fort Smith, that's where. I'm a deputy marshal, Mala, and if I don't get back from you the money you took from Miss Farthing, you're going to spend some time in that jail while you wait to stand trial on a larceny charge."

"You lawmen are all alike," she cried. "Arrogant! Officious! And not above taking bribes as your colleague, Captain Varnum of the Cherokee Lighthorse, did."

"You know about Varnum?"

"The Lowara speak of him and of the two hundred dollars in gold they were forced to pay him so that they might be allowed to remain in their camp without being troubled by him and his men."

"Well, Varnum and me, we're as unlike, I reckon, as pears and pineapples. He's—"

"You're wrong about me, you know."

"I am?"

"I wasn't trying to steal your money. What I was trying to do was put our spirits in touch with each other so that I could clearly read your future in my crystal. But when you were so close to me"—her free hand rose and began to stroke his cheek—"I was quite overcome by you. You are an overpowering man. Tell me your name."

"My name's Cimarron. Overpowering, am I?" He grinned. But he didn't release Mala.

Her hand dropped from his cheek to his chest. It wormed

102

its warm way between the buttons on his shirt and began to caress his bare chest.

The tent flap was suddenly drawn aside by a woman wearing a bird-bedecked hat and carrying a black-beaded reticule. "Excuse me. Is this where I can learn all about what fate has in store for a poor soul like me?" She blinked nervously at Mala, at Cimarron, then at both of them, her eyebrows arching in what might have been alarm.

"Come back tomorrow," Cimarron shot at her, and when she didn't immediately leave, he added, at the top of his voice, "Ten o'clock sharp!"

The woman fled, almost dropping her reticule as she did so.

"The money," Cimarron said to Mala. "Hand it over."

Mala's hand slipped from beneath his shirt and landed on the back of his neck. She drew his head down toward her and passionately kissed his lips. He tried to pull away from her, but it was a halfhearted effort that died completely when she drove her tongue into his mouth.

He nipped it with his teeth.

She shrieked.

He shook her so that her hair flew about her face. "Let's call a halt to all this chasing around the barn and get down to brass tacks. I want the eighty-seven dollars you took from Miss Farthing. Once I've got it, well, if you still want to play your game of touch and taste with me, then we can have at it. But first, the money."

Mala turned her head to one side. Between gritted teeth, she muttered, "Let me go and I'll give you the money."

He hesitated a moment and then released his hold on her.

She stepped back. "It's in a trunk, behind that curtain." She indicated the fuchsia curtain that hung behind her chair.

As she started toward it, Cimmaron took her hand and said, "We'll go get it together."

Mala swore under her breath, and then, as they reached

the curtain, she suddenly reached out with her free hand, pulled it down, and hurled it at Cimarron.

It settled on his head like a soft and gaudy cloud, and for a moment he was blinded by it. But then he tore it from his head and found that Mala had vanished. He spun around to face the entrance to the tent. He doubted that she could have gotten to the entrance and through it in the short time that he had been blinded by the curtain.

He heard a sound behind him and turned swiftly, looked down when the sound came again, and saw the lower part of Mala's legs slithering along the ground as she wriggled under the bottom of the tent. He sprang forward, bent down, and seized her ankles. He dragged her back into the tent again. But before she was all the way inside it again, she reached up and seized the tent, causing it to collapse, burying both of them beneath it as it did so.

She screamed at the top of her voice, a single word: "*Rape!*"

Cimarron, almost totally immobilized by the fallen tent, finally managed, by pushing and shoving and pulling, to get to his feet and free himself of it.

Mala was a squirming bundle beneath the tent's thick canvas as she rose, fell, rose, and fell again, cursing him all the while in both English and Romany.

Cimarron tore at the canvas and finally uncovered her. He had no sooner done so than she again screamed, "*Rape!*"

A moment later, as he stared at her in utter amazement and she pointed an accusing finger at him and let loose a torrent of words in the Romany language, he felt himself seized from behind and hauled to his feet. Before he could defend himself, his arms were pinioned behind his back.

Mala slowly got to her feet. She whimpered. She wept.

Women ran to her aid.

"What is this?" Luluvo asked as he appeared to confront Cimarron, his face grave, his eyes dark. "What have you done?"

Cimarron tried and failed to break the grip of the man who was immobilizing his arms behind his back. He re-

minded Luluvo of how Mala had deceived Serena Farthing in Muskogee and made off with eighty-seven dollars
of her money. "I came here and I told Mala I was fixing to
arrest her if she didn't hand over that money she ran off
with. She wouldn't. She tried to make a run for it. I went
after her. The tent fell down on top of us. That's what
happened. Not what she's been yelling about. *That* never
happened between her and me!"

"Mala?" Luluvo turned to face her.

She shook her head, tears still oozing from her eyes,
and then spoke in a subdued voice and at some length to
Luluvo in their language.

When she had finished, he turned back to Cimarron.
"Mala claims she was never in Muskogee, that she knows
no woman named Serena Farthing, that you came to her
tent and offered to pay her to have relations with you.
When she wouldn't, she says you tried to take her by
force."

"She's a goddamned liar is what she is," Cimarron bellowed indignantly.

Kore suddenly materialized out of the crowd, his hair
disheveled, a cut beneath his left eye on which dried
blood had crusted, the skin scraped from his knuckles. He
stood glaring at Cimarron as the other gypsies, both Lowara
and Tshurara, withdrew from him.

"That slut Rupa has made me unclean," he stated flatly.
"I therefore have the right to call the *kris* into session to
hear my side of the story of the relationship between me
and that deputy marshal so that Rupa's curse may be lifted
from me and I may become once again clean and whole-
some.

"I ask for the *kris* for another reason as well. Our gypsy
court must convene and pass judgment on this *gajo* for
what he has done to my woman."

"Your woman!" Cimarron heard himself say, surprise
sharpening his tone.

"Kore and Mala are husband and wife," Luluvo explained.

"Am I not right?" Kore asked the gathered gypsies.

"Should not the *kris* pass judgment upon me and upon him?" His index finger shot out as if to impale Cimarron.

Murmurs ran through the crowd. Voices were raised in favor of convening the *kris*, the court of the gypsies. Someone angrily denounced Cimarron. Someone else spoke harshly of Rupa and how she had earlier made Kore *marhimé*.

Luluvo raised a hand, and silence descended upon the crowd. "I will take under consideration Kore's request for the convening of the *kris*. As for this man here"—he indicated Cimarron—"he is not one of us. Let him go."

The man holding Cimarron released him.

Cimarron flexed his arms to restore circulation to them as he stared angrily at Kore. Then, shifting his gaze to Luluvo, he said in a flat voice, "I got this to say to you, Luluvo. To all of you. I didn't molest Mala and that's the truth no matter what lies she tries to tell you all.

"And another thing. Some of you know I'm a lawman. Well, it's my job to take Mala to Fort Smith to stand trial for larceny and I'm going to do it."

"You're not!" Luluvo had spoken in an icy voice, and as if his words had been a signal to the other gypsies, clubs suddenly appeared in the hands of some, revolvers and knives in the hands of others. The mob of gypsies advanced menacingly on Cimarron, but Luluvo held up a hand to stay them.

"*Gajo* law is not our law," he told Cimarron. "You will not take one of our own without a battle in which, should you choose to use your gun, outnumbered by us as you are, you would surely die. That would be a sad and unnecessary thing. So go away from us, Cimarron, and do not come back. We took you for a friend and you turned on us like a rabid dog. You attacked one of our women, disgracing her and all of us as well."

"I told you what really happened," Cimarron protested. "And what I told you's the truth! Mala's been lying to you!"

"Go, Cimarron," Luluvo persisted. "Take your horse

and ride away from here. You have betrayed the friend-ship the Rom offered you."

Cimarron was about to argue against Luluvo's harsh judgment of him, but seeing Kore's malevolent eyes fixed upon him and seeing Mala's mocking smile, he hesitated. He surveyed the crowd facing him and knew he could not battle such a mob single-handedly. He caught Rupa's eye but she turned her back to him.

He shrugged and made his way to his bay. After freeing the horse from the tree to which he had tethered it when he returned from buying his new hat in Locust Grove, he swung into the saddle and rode away.

The sun was setting when Cimarron, riding due east, arrived at the town of Oaks in Cherokee Nation. As he rode down the dusty main street, the glass in the windows of the stores lining it were turned to sheets of gold by the slanting rays of the setting sun. He drew rein in front of a building that bore a sign proclaiming it a restaurant, dis-mounted, and tethered his horse to the hitchrail in front of the building.

He entered the restaurant, took a table against one wall from which he could see both the front door and the one leading, presumably, to the kitchen in the rear of the building. When a Cherokee waiter appeared before him, he ordered a beefsteak, boiled potatoes, bread, and coffee.

He was eating the meal that had been brought to him when four men, all of them Cherokees and all of them drunk, staggered into the restaurant and sank into chairs at an empty table next to Cimarron's.

He forked the last of his potatoes into his mouth and then proceeded to spread butter on a thick slice of bread that he soaked in his coffee before devouring.

Snatches of conversation from the drunken Indians reached him as he buttered a second piece of bread and used it to mop up the bloody juices on his plate.

"—but it's not booger dancing we ought to be doing, it's scalp dancing."

"Damn right!"

"Damn gypsies . . . kill every last one of them . . ."

One of the men laughed hilariously at something Cimarron had not heard, his head thrown back, both of his hands clasped about his ample girth. Then, catching Cimarron's eye, he asked, "What's your opinion of the matter, mister?"

"What matter?" Cimarron asked, his curiosity aroused by the reference to gypsies.

"White men like him," growled a second Cherokee at the table, "they hate those gypsies every bit as much as us Indians do, and for the same damn good reasons. Because gypsies—every mother's son of them—steal, cheat, carry off children—"

"What do you say, mister?" prodded the Cherokee who had first spoken to Cimarron. "By the way, my name's Burke."

Cimarron briefly considered the kind of answer he should give Burke and then made his choice, which he hoped his hearers would find provocative. "A mortal enemy of mine happens to be a gypsy name of Kore."

"He's one with us!" crowed the big-bellied Burke as he reached out and enthusiastically shook Cimarron's hand. Then, frowning and turning back to his three companions, he boomed, "To hell with booger dancing. What we ought to be doing is scalp dancing, like I said before. Like we used to do in the good old days back East. Now, my pappy's got some Creek scalps stored away in a trunk up in our attic; he took them when he was a youngster. What say I go get them and we show those Indians over at the meeting hall the way Cherokee warriors can dance?"

Cheers rose from the throats of Burke's three companions and then they all rose and made for the door.

When they had gone, Cimarron beckoned to the waiter, who approached his table, shaking his head. "How much?" he asked, and when the man had told him the cost of his meal, he paid for it and then, as the waiter was about to return to the kitchen, asked, "Those men who just left— what was all that talk of theirs about, do you know?"

"There were some gypsies who came through town not

108

long ago," the waiter replied. "They stole practically everything that wasn't nailed down. Made a lot of folks mad, those devils did. I guess those men are bent on bringing back the old scalp dance."

"What's it and its purpose?"

"It was a warriors' dance in the old days; the men danced and boasted of their exploits in war—how many scalps they took, how long their battles lasted, that sort of thing. It was often used to fire up the other men, most especially the young ones to get them to want to go out on the warpath against their enemies, which in the case of us Cherokees was usually the Creeks."

"You folks are having some kind of a dance tonight, are you?"

"Yes, a booger dance, in the meeting hall across the street. It's a dance we believe can weaken the harmful powers of our enemies who might cause us harm. We believe it makes them powerless against us, without causing bloodshed."

Looks like some folks want a scalp dance instead, Cimarron thought as he rose from the table, bade good night to the waiter, and left the restaurant. He cut diagonally across the street, heading for the building marked MEETING HALL, from which wild whoops and wilder music were coming.

7

As he entered the meeting hall, Cimarron found himself in the midst of a dense crowd of people in a circle around dancers in the center of the huge room. The dancers were circling a corn mortar that had been overturned and placed in the middle of the floor.

A drum made of a section of buckeye trunk dyed with red clay and stained with sumach berries sounded as a Cherokee, seated cross-legged on the floor with the drum before him, pounded on its woodchuck-skin covering which was held firmly in place by a taut hoop of hickory. Many of the dancers wore grotesque masks with wildly exaggerated features stained red and brown and black. They moved in a counterclockwise direction following the leader of the dance. Their bodies were draped in either ragged blankets or shredded clothes.

Some of them carried gourd hand rattles that they shook as they shuffled along, one behind the other. Among the dancers were several women, all of whom wore tortoise-shell rattles bound to their legs. The rattles added to the din made by the drum, and it was augmented by the occasional high-pitched yells and loud growls emitted by the dancers.

Cimarron turned his attention from the dancers to the crowd lining all four sides of the room. Cherokees, every

110

last one of them, he observed. But they don't look like they're ready to hit the warpath. They look like they're having way too good a time right here.

There were smiles on many of the spectators' faces. Some clapped their hands in delight as they watched one of the dancers who had distorted his figure by stuffing his clothes, thereby grotesquely distending his abdomen.

Cimarron also watched as the man, who was now avidly dancing, suddenly whipped out from beneath the torn sheet draped over his body a long gourd that resembled an erect male member. The dancer dashed to the side-lines, upended his gourd, and poured the water it contained down upon a gaily shrieking cluster of young Cherokee women.

"Three cheers for Big Balls!" someone shouted, and the crowd obediently responded with three lusty cheers which elicited a melodramatic bow from the dancer with the gourd-phallus in his hand, who then rejoined the long line of dancers.

"What kind of a name is that?" Cimarron asked a young Cherokee standing next to him. "Big Balls, I mean?"

"All the men dancing take obscene names like that," responded the young man. "For the purposes of the booger dance, that is. See that man there." He pointed. "He is called Burster and I'll bet you can guess what it is he bursts and with what he bursts it." The man smiled. "That man"—he pointed to a dancer just behind the young leader—"he is called Sooty Ass and the one behind him, Black Buttocks."

"What's this here booger dance all about?" Cimarron asked his eager informant.

The young man's answer was drowned out by loud applause from the crowd, clearly signaling their appreciation of the dancer named Black Buttocks, who had just turned his back on the crowd and flipped up his ragged blanket to reveal a blackened behind beneath his torn trousers. Cimarron repeated his question as Burster seized a young and comely woman, lifted her off the floor, and planted a loud kiss on her cheek before setting her down again and rejoining the dance.

"We hold a booger dance," the young man replied, tapping his foot in time to the buckeye drum's rhythm, "to weaken the powers of enemy tribes who would cause us misfortune or harm."

"What enemies do you happen to have in mind, if you don't mind my asking?"

The young man launched into a long and bitter denunciation of gypsies in general, and those who had recently visited the town of Oaks in particular, his tirade punctuated with obscenities and characterized by an angry passion only barely kept within bounds.

"I heard—" Cimarron never got to finish whatever it was he had been about to say because, at that moment, the four Cherokees he had seen earlier in the restaurant burst through the front door of the meeting hall, yelling at the top of their voices and brandishing in their hands what he immediately recognized as ancient and desiccated scalps.

Waving eagle-feather wands along with the scalps, the four men quickly chased the other dancers from the floor and they blended into the crowd of spectators.

The man who had introduced himself as Burke in the restaurant beckoned to the drummer, who rose and joined him. The two men conversed briefly and then Burke exhorted the watching throng. "Join us, you men, in the scalp dance of our ancestors. Not for us—nor for you, I hope—is the booger dance, which may or may not be effective in weakening the power of the gypsies. We will dance the scalp dance! Come and dance with us!"

Cimarron watched as the four men, each of whom had an eagle-feather wand in his right hand and a scalp in his left hand, began to circle the large empty space in the center of the meeting hall.

"*He ha li!*" sang the man with the drum as he beat it, and took up a position in the middle of the line formed by the four dancing men.

"*Ye ye!*" shouted the dancers in response.

After the five had circled the hall several times, the

singing ceased and the drummer withdrew from the line. The remaining men walked slowly around the room, the man in the lead—Burke—began to declaim his valor and his willingness to make war on the gypsies.

"Let them tremble in fear at our coming, for we are strong and willing warriors and we will take their hair to keep them from doing any more harm to us. We will fight the gypsies and we will win. We will be brave and we will die, if we must, to save our people from the wiles and wickednesses of those evil-eyed fiends who have been preying upon us."

Burke then stepped aside and the man behind him bellowed, "No punishment is too severe for the gypsies who torment us. Death must be their lot and we will bring it to them with shouts of joy on our lips and a burning hate in our hearts. Those who have harmed us by their thieving, their rapaciousness with our women, and their blasphemies in daring to foretell the future that should be known only to God will be killed." He dramatically flourished both the eagle-feather wand and the scalp he held in his hands.

Cimarron listened as the man ranted and raved on. He suppressed a smile as the next man in line did the same, proclaiming himself fearless and eager to die in a cause he called sacred: "The extermination of the gypsy vermin who have come to infest the homelands of the Cherokee people."

But Cimarron felt no urge to smile as other men, most of them young, joined the first four dancers and added their whoops and loud shouts to those punctuating the beginning and end of each dancer's recitation of his eager intent to wreak havoc upon the gypsies.

He became at first uneasy as time passed and more men joined the scalp dance, and then decidedly apprehensive as the dancers shook their fists in the air and shouted vehement denunciations of the gypsies, whom they all vowed first to kill and then to scalp.

But all this, he told himself, is none of my affair. Especially not now, since Luluvo sent me packing. This here's strictly between the gypsies and the Cherokees. It's no skin off my ass if these Cherokees wind up scalping every last gypsy between here and the Rockies.

An image of Rupa flickered briefly in his mind and then was gone.

He gnawed his lower lip, thinking, Those gypsies, they sentenced you. Forget them. Let them go their way and you go yours. And let the Cherokees—

Rupa returned, a dazzling vision of dark loveliness in his mind's eyes, and despite himself, he saw her scalped and badly bleeding. Her eyes pleaded with him, but she was unable to speak his name or ask his help because the scalp dancers had cut out her tongue . . .

But the Lowara want no part of me, he told himself angrily. And the Tshurara would as soon kill me as kick me. Not a one of them would even hear my side of the story, only Mala's. They're fools, is what they are, those goddamned gypsies! Worse than fools! They're villains who judge a man without fully considering all the facts in his case. They get their exercise jumping to faulty conclusions. So to hell with them!

"Flay them alive, that's what we should do!" cried a young man who had joined the scalp dancers. "They told me my wife made me a cuckold and I beat her for it, but she was innocent. She proved to me that the gypsy woman had told me a lie. So let us stamp them out—them and the discord they seek to sow among us God-fearing folk!"

But Luluvo, Cimarron thought, when I was blinded and hurt so bad, he volunteered to take me to Fort Smith even though he and his people had been intending to head north, not east. That ought to count for something, he thought, and never mind that later he wouldn't believe what I said happened between me and Mala.

Remembering the aged gypsy's earlier kindness and generosity, and successfully suppressing his anger over the fact that Luluvo had believed Mala's lies and not the truth he had told the old man, Cimarron turned on his heels and left the meeting hall.

Outside, he crossed the street to where he had left his bay in front of the restaurant. He freed the animal from

114

the hitchrail, swung into the saddle, and rode out of Oaks, heading back to the camp of the Lowara gypsies.

Cimarron heard the riders coming toward him long before he could see them because night had fallen and the half-moon in the sky above him shed little light. He turned his horse, intending to head for a stand of sycamores on one side of the trail he was traveling to Locust Grove, when someone, just a shadow in the night, shouted, "There he is!"

He never made it to the sycamores. Within seconds, he found himself surrounded by a horde of gypsies on horseback, all of them armed in one way or another—with guns, with knives, with clubs. He recognized them as Lowara gypsies in the dim white light of the moon. But the only man present whose name he knew was Yayal, who at the trading fair had managed to sell his aging horse to an unsuspecting *gajo* by making it seem spirited.

"We got him!" exulted one of the men in the crowd, brandishing a six-gun at Cimarron.

"What the hell's this all about?" Cimarron barked, his eyes roving from face to face as the men glared menacingly at him. "What the hell are you night riders up to?"

"Follow me," one of the gypsies directed before turning his mount and riding back the way he had come.

As the other gypsies closed ranks on his flanks and directly behind him, Cimarron saw that he had no choice but to follow the leader of the band, who was riding west. He did so, and when he and the others reached the gypsy camp north of Locust Grove, he saw a group of men seated on boxes and trunks near a huge campfire from which sparks darted up into the sky.

He was prodded by gun muzzles and wooden clubs toward the men and the fire, and when he reached them, he was ordered to dismount, which he did.

Luluvo, he was able to see now, was one of the several men seated near the fire. He spotted Kore standing some distance away from the men. Neither Kore nor Luluvo looked in his direction.

"She defiled me on purpose," Kore stated, addressing Luluvo and the men with him. "Rupa is the one who deserves banishment, not me."

"Rupa did what she did," Luluvo declared, "to stop you from fighting."

"Sure, I was fighting," Kore admitted in response to Luluvo's implied criticism. "But I didn't start the fight. He did!" Kore acknowledged Cimarron's presence for the first time with a curt nod in his direction.

"But you and your men attacked Cimarron in the north when he went there to talk to Mala," Luluvo pointed out.

"I had to defend my wife from him," Kore countered, anger giving a sharp edge to his voice. "But what's at issue here is my claim that I was treated unjustly by Rupa and that I deserve to have the ritual defilement lifted by you, the *krisatora* of the *kris*, the judges of the court."

Luluvo conferred in whispers with the men seated on either side of him, and then, after several minutes of subdued arguing, he turned back to Kore. "It is the decision of the *krisatora*—both those from the Lowara tribe and those who are Tshurara—that the ritual defilement you have suffered as a result of Rupa's actions be lifted. Although what you did to Cimarron cannot be entirely condoned, nevertheless the *krisatora* feel that you have been made to suffer unduly as a result of what Rupa did to you."

Kore let out a whoop of joy and then sprang forward and vigorously pumped the hands of his judges, thanking each of them profusely, before turning around to stare at Cimarron, his hands planted jauntily on his hips, as if daring him to contest the judgment of the *kris*.

Cimarron ignored him. Addressing Luluvo, who now sat staring moodily into the fire, he said, "First you went and ran me off. Then you send out your boys to drag me back. Luluvo, would you mind all that much telling me just exactly what the hell's going on?"

Luluvo slowly turned on his seat to face Cimarron. There was sorrow in his eyes and his voice was melancholy when he answered, "I sent you away from us without subjecting you to the jugment of the *kris*—when you tried to rape Mala. But now—" Luluvo looked heavenward as if seeking help from that quarter, before returning his attention to Cimarron. "Now, we have no choice but to try you for a most heinous crime committed against us."

"Hold on there," Cimarron said sharply. "Am I to take it that you're accusing me of committing some kind of crime?"

Luluvo nodded.

"What crime?"

"Murder." The ugly word Luluvo had uttered was a knife stabbing the heart of the dark night.

"Murder?" Cimarron repeated in disbelief. "You mean to say you're accusing me of murdering somebody, Luluvo?"

"Mala."

"Mala's been murdered?"

Luluvo nodded.

"When?"

"Earlier this evening. Shortly after we sent you away from the camp."

"Then you can't blame me for killing her," Cimarron declared triumphantly. "After I left here, I rode straight to Oaks on my way back to Fort Smith. Folks saw me there. They'll say they did. If Mala was murdered when you say she was, you can't lay the blame for what happened on my doorstep on account of I wasn't anywhere around here when you say she was killed."

"You could have come back after leaving our camp, done the evil deed, and then rode quickly to Oaks in order to establish an alibi for yourself," Luluvo stated in the same melancholy tone he had used earlier.

Cimarron started to protest, but Luluvo, interrupting him, ordered the men surrounding Cimarron to lead him to a spot where he could directly face the *krisatora*.

When two men seized Cimarron's arms to obey Luluvo's order, he shook himself free of them and strode alone to the spot Luluvo had indicated.

"Now, then," he said, trying to keep the anger and uneasiness he was feeling from his voice. "What proof

117

have you got that makes you think I'm the one who murdered Mala?"

"She accused you," Luluvo replied solemnly, "before she died."

Cimarron, taken aback by Luluvo's words, hesitated a moment and then, "Maybe you'd better tell me what exactly happened."

"I found Mala when I returned to my wagon just after dark. She was lying outside it. She had been struck on the head with a hammer that had been taken from my wagon. I knew at once that she was dying, and so did the others when they came upon us there.

"I asked her who had done the terrible thing to her. She could barely speak. But she did manage to utter two words."

When Luluvo paused as if weary, Cimarron asked, "What two words?"

"In answer to my question," Luluvo said, his eyes boring into Cimarron's, she replied, " 'The lawman.' "

Cimarron's teeth ground together.

"I asked Mala why she had been struck. At first, she could not answer me because of the blood that began to bubble from between her lips." Luluvo dropped his head in his hands and was silent for a long moment. Then, looking up again, he continued, "I wiped the blood from her lips and she whispered, 'He wanted the money.' "

Cimarron heard the angry muttering that ran through the crowd of gypsies and he noted the dark looks the *krisatora* seated on either side of Luluvo were giving him. He was about to speak when one of the *krisatora* beckoned and a man emerged from the crowd. Cimarron watched the man bend down and spread a brightly colored green kerchief on the ground midway between where he stood and the *krisatora* sat. He continued watching as the man placed upon the kerchief a crudely carved cross, then a faded photograph of Mala, and finally a small bunch of golden chrysanthemums.

He took a white candle stump from his pocket, lit it,

and placed it upright on the ground beside the collection of objects resting on the kerchief.

As he melted back into the crowd, Luluvo looked directly at Cimarron and said, "Now the *solakh*, the truth-seeking, will begin. The accused still has time to admit his guilt. You see there on the ground before you, Cimarron, the cut flowers which, for the Rom, symbolize premature death, as in Mala's sad case. We ask you to look at her photograph. We ask you by the power of the cross that saves the souls of sinners such as yourself—"

"Wait one goddamned minute!" Cimarron roared. "You sound like you've gone and already convicted me without me ever having a chance to even offer any kind of defense! What kind of a judicial proceeding is this?"

"—to confess to your dastardly crime," Luluvo continued, completely unperturbed by Cimarron's outburst. "If you do not, will not, confess your crime, we shall, by our collective will, summon the *mulé*, the spirits of the dead, and they will, through the power of their awesome magic, force you to confess."

"I'm not confessing to anything I didn't do, and that includes the murder of Mala," Cimarron bellowed. "In fact, I'm fed up to here with this whole show and don't intend to keep on being part of it."

He turned and strode away. But he had gone no more than a few steps when he was jumped by five gypsy men who brought him down to the ground. He was quickly overpowered and then roughly hauled to his feet, his hands now tightly bound behind his back. The men who had downed him formed a phalanx around him, clearly intending to prevent him from making a second attempt to leave the camp.

Luluvo took several steps in his direction. "If you know or have heard anything related to the death of Mala and you do not so inform this *kris*, then may you die in horrible agony."

"*Bater*." The word rose from the throats of many of the watching gypsies together with what Cimarron assumed was its English translation: "May it be so."

"If, in any even remote way, you have had any connection with the murder of Mala, may noxious and evil winds hit your belly and render you ill with a deadly disease."

"*Bater.*" The word drifted in the air around Cimarron. Luluvo continued speaking, almost chanting, and the curses he was pronouncing grew more terrible and more merciless, the questions he put to Cimarron more complex and more subtle.

Between the two men the flame of the candle guttered on the ground in a light breeze that had arisen.

When Luluvo finally fell silent, Cimarron met his steady gaze and stated flatly, "I don't know whether you folks are expecting me to be struck dead by a thunderbolt or something, but if you do, you're all in for a big disappointment. I didn't kill Mala. And there's no way in this wide world that you can prove I did!"

"Murderer!"

Cimarron glanced to one side and saw Kore, his face contorted, his eyes wild, as he shouted, "Murderer!" a second time and pointed an accusing finger at Cimarron. "My beloved named her murderer before she died," he screeched, tears streaming down his cheeks. "That deputy standing there was determined to get from her the money he claimed she stole from a woman in Muskogee. When she would not give it to him—because she did not steal it—he returned like a thief in the night, and when she still refused to give him any money, he struck her with a hammer he took from Luluvo's wagon."

"I never once set foot inside Luluvo's wagon," Cimarron shot back. "Not ever!"

"Mala's spilled blood calls out to the Rom for vengeance!" Kore screamed. He threw back his head and raised both fisted hands to the night sky. "Kill him!"

Cimarron, still surrounded by gypsies who enclosed him like the bars of a living prison, watched as Luluvo consulted in hushed tones with his fellow judges. Their conference lasted no more than four or five minutes, but to him it seemed an eternity.

At last, Luluvo turned back to face Cimarron. "We

krisatora have reached a decision in this grave matter. We find the man named Cimarron guilty of the crime of which he has been accused because Mala's dying words indict him. He must pay for his crime and we will see to it that he does pay. At the first light of day, he will be taken to a place of punishment where he will pay with his life for what he has done.

"But now, as is our custom, we will first forgive the one who has transgressed against us." Gazing into Cimarron's narrowed eyes, Luluvo intoned, *"Te aves yetime mader tai te yertil tut of Del."* He drew a deep breath and murmured, "I forgive you and may God forgive you as I do."

Dawn found Cimarron lying shirtless on his back on the ground some distance from the camp of the Lowara. His wrists were tightly tied with rawhide thongs to stakes that had been driven into the ground, his arms forming a wide-angled V above his head. His legs were also spread-eagled, his ankles bound to two more stakes, so that they formed an inverted V.

He began to squirm, straining against the rawhide thongs that bound him so securely. But neither they nor the stakes gave way.

He stared up at the gypsies gathered around him, Luluvo and Kore among them, and as he did so, he became aware of something moving beneath his bare back. His skin began to crawl and then he grunted as something bit him in the small of his back. The ground beneath him suddenly seemed alive. It seemed to him to be moving. And then, as he saw the first of the tiny red insects swarming across his naked chest, he realized that the gypsies had staked him out over a red ant hill. He flinched as one of the ants bit into the exposed flesh of his belly.

Luluvo spoke to him then in a funereal tone. "We will leave your horse here to die with you." He pointed, and Cimarron turned his head in the direction of his bay, which had been tethered to a nearby pin oak. "The animal will die of starvation as will you, unless the ants kill you first, as well they might. Their pincers are small but they are powerful. In time, you will wish that you could reach your gun so you could use it to put an end to your agony."

A shadow fell across Cimarron as Luluvo bent down, a honeycomb in his hand. He smeared some of the honey from the comb on Cimarron's chest and said, "You are far from any trail and even farther from any town or dwelling. If you cry out for help, no one will hear you." He straightened and dropped the honeycomb beside Cimarron's shirt and bandanna, which lay nearby on the ground.

"It is not enough," a voice protested loudly.

Cimarron turned his head and saw Kore, his eyes afire, glaring at Luluvo. "Someone may come this way and free him. The ants may go away before they have killed him. He might be discovered by someone passing through here before he has starved to death."

Luluvo, confronting the angry Kore, said, "This is the sentence passed by the *krisatora*. It is a just one. You have no right to interfere with it."

Kore's hand eased toward the six-gun he wore strapped around his waist.

At a signal from Luluvo, several of the Lowara men surrounded Kore as they had surrounded Cimarron.

Luluvo said, "We go now. Come with us, Kore."

Cimarron watched as the Lowara escorted the grim-faced Kore away from the scene in obedience to Luluvo's command, spoken so softly it might have been merely a request.

In the silence following the departure of the Lowara, Cimarron stared up at the sky, which dawn was brightening. Involuntary spasms racked his body as his muscles reacted to the depredations of the ants swarming over his chest to feed on the honey covering it.

He tried again to pull one of the stakes from the ground, and failed to do so. He soon found that he could move none of them, not even as much as a fraction of an inch. He lay there sweating as the sun rose in the sky, almost becoming accustomed to the sharp and constant nipping of the ants' mandibles as they tore at his chest, his belly, his face.

By the time the sun had reached its zenith, he wanted desperately to scream and to find in that scream at least momentary relief from the pain that was ripping through him in a wild red tide to match the relentless red tide of ants that were feeding on his flesh.

He twisted his head and stared at the rawhide thong that bound his right wrist. As he stared helplessly at it, he found himself imagining the hopeless animal to which that leathery flesh had once belonged. Sweat slid into his eyes, momentarily blinding him. When he could see again, he noticed the honeycomb lying nearby, the honeycomb Luluvo had dropped.

His eyes moved between the comb and the rawhide binding his wrist. He looked down at the ants that were eagerly devouring him, their bites like the painful punctures of hundreds of sharp needles. He stared grimly at the blood that was seeping from the shredded skin of his chest and then looked around him, turning his head first one way and then the other.

Stones littered the ground. Clumps of frost-stricken grass were everywhere. A stunted juniper grew not far away.

He stared at the gnarled plant for a moment and then eased his body to the right. Straining hard, the cords in his neck standing out in stiff ridges, he stretched even more until he thought his neck would break.

At last, after many long minutes, his teeth closed on a branch of the juniper bush and he bit down hard, snapping it. His head jerked back and his muscles relaxed. He raised his head, and as he carefully swept the juniper branch across his chest, it picked up ants and honey. He turned his head, strained again as hard as he could, and barely managed to brush the juniper against the rawhide that was restraining his right wrist, depositing honey and ants upon it.

Working steadily, he repeated what he had done several more times, and when he had finished, his teeth released the juniper branch and it fell to the ground by his side. He watched the ants begin to attack the leather he had swabbed with the honey.

Time passed, and Cimarron would not allow himself to hope. He merely continued to stare steadily at the ants that were biting into his wrist and into the leather that bound it to the stake.

More time passed and some of the ants began to crawl back along his arm, heading for his chest and what honey remained there. As more and more of the ants abandoned the leather that was no longer sticky with honey because the ants had devoured it all, he twisted his wrist, first to the right and then to the left.

It remained bound to the stake. And he remained a victim of the ants that were still feasting on his body and his blood.

He tried again. He twisted his wrist and then jerked it as hard as he could, the muscles in his arm knotted and anguished by the supreme effort he was making. Blood began to boom in his temples. His vision blurred as sweat from his forehead oozed into his eyes. He wanted to rest but he wouldn't let himself do so.

One more time, he thought. Third time's the charm. *It's got to be!*

His arm strained as he struggled to break free. For one awful moment, he thought his wrist was about to shatter. But then the thong snapped.

As his wrist fell free, he lay on the ground panting, barely aware of the pain the ants were causing him, almost grateful to them for the way they had, while devouring the honey he had daubed on the leather, bitten through it in places just as they had bitten into his body, weakening the rawhide sufficiently so that he was finally able to tear it.

He clawed ants from his face with his free hand and then quickly untied the thong that bound his left wrist. Then, sitting up, he scraped away the living carpet of red ants covering his chest and proceeded to free his feet.

Flooded with a feeling of relief, he got to his feet and stood there, swaying unsteadily, his head spinning and his body racked by the pain of the ordeal he had just undergone.

As he bent down to pick up his shirt and bandanna, he

almost lost his balance as a wave of dizziness swept over him. He straightened and, carrying his shirt and bandanna, went to his bay.

"Well, old son," he whispered to the horse as he freed it and began to lead it away, "it does look like neither one of us is going to starve to death, or, in my case, get himself eaten up alive by that bunch of red ants that makes its home over yonder."

He led the bay to a small stream, a tributary of the Grand River, and as the horse dropped its head to drink, he knelt on the bank next to the animal and used his bandanna, which he soaked in the stream's cold water, as a sponge to rid his chest and face of their slick coating of blood. Then he too drank deeply before standing up and putting on his shirt. He pulled the bay's head up, not wanting to let the animal drink too much until he was sure he could let it rest. He was about to climb into the saddle when he saw the riders bearing down on him.

He went for his gun, but a warning shot fired by one of the mounted men whistled past his left ear, stopping his hand in midair. And then they were pulling up and drawing rein around him, and he recognized them as Tshurara gypsies who were being led by the angry-eyed Kore.

Kore muttered an obscenity.

"You were right," one of his riders said to him. "The *krisatora* should have ordered this lawman shot dead instead of what they did do to him."

"Dead men don't have a chance to escape," stated another man from behind Kore.

"The *krisatora*," Kore declared, his voice chilly, "are foolish old men. They fear death and dying, and so they shrink from shedding blood by their own hands. But the Tshurara do not fear death or dying, nor do we shrink from the shedding of blood."

"You brought us here to finish off the lawman," one of Kore's riders reminded him. "Let's do it!"

Kore held up a hand. "We could shoot him dead right where he stands," he mused in an icy tone. "Or we could . . ." His words faded away.

The rider on his right said, "Come on, Kore. Tell us just exactly what we're going to do to this deputy."

"Something special," Kore responded. "Something real special. Something he's not going to like the least little bit. That's what we're going to do with this lawman."

8

Cimarron sat on the ground late that night in the winter camp of the Tshurara, his back braced against the trunk of an elm, his arms wrapped around it, and his hands tightly tied with a length of rope behind it. He stared morosely at the gypsies who were gathered around a blazing campfire in the distance. The sound of Kore's voice, borne by the wind, drifted to him.

"In the morning, half of you will go to Salina, the other half to Oaks, as you did yesterday and the day before. Once there, you will once again work your wiles on shop-keepers and merchants. You will steal every penny you can from their tills. You will take with you our false-bottomed containers, which you will fill with food and other items of value. The women will make themselves friendly with the men in Salina and Oaks, but friendlier still with their wallets, which they will appropriate while the *gaje* are under the spell of their feminine charms.

"A few of you men will go to the banks. Once there, some of you will distract the tellers so that the others can steal the money in the cash drawers while no one is looking. Make sure, all of you, that you are as sly as foxes and as quick as rabbits as you go about your business."

As Kore continued instructing the Tshurara men and women, Cimarron glanced to the left where his bay stood tethered to a rope strung between two trees along with the mounts of the gypsies. His eyes lingered longingly on his cartridge belt, which Kore had taken from him and draped over his saddle, his .44 hanging from it in its oiled holster. My horse and my gun are near enough to me, he thought. But tied up like I am they might just as well be a million miles away.

He twisted his wrists in an effort to free himself, but the rope that bound them did not give. He tried tightening his right hand, making it as small as he possibly could, in the hope that he could then pull it through the encircling rope. But his effort failed because the rope was tied too tightly. He stiffened and glanced to the right as he heard someone approaching him.

He stared at the full-skirted gypsy woman who was walking hurriedly toward him, one hand clutching a heavy shawl she had wrapped around her head and shoulders, a plate of food in her other hand. She stopped in front of him and then looked back over her shoulder toward the gypsies gathered by the fire.

"I'm not hungry, honey," he told her. "And were I, well, you'd have to feed me, seeing as how my hands, tied up like they are, aren't of any use to me at the moment."

To his surprise, instead of speaking to him or offering him the plate of food, the woman, whose face he could not see because it was shadowed by her shawl, set down the plate and darted behind the trunk of the tree to which he was bound.

"Did I scare you?" he whispered, twisting his head in an attempt to see where she had gone. "Hey, honey, where'd you disappear to?"

When he got no answer, he shrugged, deciding that the woman, for whatever reason of her own, had, instead of feeding him, fled into the woods behind him. And then, to his complete surprise, he felt soft hands touch his wrists, and to his even greater surprise, he felt the blade of a knife moments later nick his left wrist as someone began to cut his bonds.

"Honey?"

"Quiet!"

He knew the voice and yet he couldn't believe he had heard correctly. What was she doing here in the camp of the Tshurara? He hadn't seen her since . . . When was the last time? Before he had stood trial at the hands of the *krisatora*. "Rupa?" he whispered. "It really is you?"

"Hush!"

He shook his head in wonderment. "What the hell— beg pardon, Rupa—but what are you doing here?"

"Isn't it obvious?" she murmured as she cut the last strand of the rope that kept him prisoner.

Quickly, he eased around behind the tree. And there she was on her knees, the shawl fallen from her head to rest on her shoulders. Rupa.

He kissed her. "I sure am glad to see you, honey. But what—how—?"

She shook her head and frowned to silence him. "I couldn't bear the thought of you suffering what the *kris* had decreed was to be your fate. I waited until the camp was asleep and then I rode out to the place where they had taken you. But you were gone. I heard noises in the distance, near the stream. I went to investigate and saw Kore and his men, and you. I realized what must have happened."

"They got the drop on me. Took me prisoner. Brought me here."

"I know. I followed you. Then, when the Tshurara were talking over there, I pulled my shawl over my head, stole a plate of food from a wagon, and made my way here to you."

"They could have spotted you."

"It was a risk, but one I thought was worth taking."

Cimarron kissed her a second time.

"They wouldn't pay too much attention to me, I thought. They have other things on their mind at the moment. And after all, what is one more gypsy woman in the camp of the Tshurara. But now—" Rupa peered around the trunk of the tree at the campfire and the gypsies who were gathered around it, "—we must go."

"My horse," Cimarron said, "he's right over there. I'll go get him. Where'd you leave your mount?"

"On the south side of the camp. I'll work my way around the camp. I'll go through the woods. You get your horse."

"And I'll do the same thing and meet you south of here."

He was just about to kiss Rupa a third time but she rose and vanished into the darkness of the forest. He rose and ran stealthily through the trees until he reached the spot where his horse was tethered. He freed the bay and, after strapping his cartridge belt around his hips, led it through the woods as he made his way south. When the light of the Tshurara tribe's fire could no longer be seen behind him, he halted and squinted through the trees; they stood like nearly leafless sentinels as they waited the arrival of another winter. But he could see Rupa nowhere.

He looked up at the polestar, and because of its position in the sky, he knew that he had not lost his way, that he had headed south to the planned rendezvous with Rupa as he had indeed intended to do. Then, where was she? He led the bay to the left, and after walking for some distance in that direction, he retraced his steps and headed back in the opposite direction. Soon after he had passed the spot from which he had started, he heard movement in the darkness and he halted, tensing and peering into the gloom.

"Cimarron?"

Rupa had whispered his name in a faint, almost inaudible voice tinged with apprehension.

"It's me. Where are you?"

"Here."

He turned and headed in the direction from which her voice had come. He moved cautiously, his hand on his bridle chains to keep them from jingling, trying to make no noise, or at least as little as possible. He had not gone far when he heard a twig snap behind him. His first thought was that he had passed Rupa in the darkness. His second, as he heard someone moving up on him fast from behind, was that the someone he had heard was moving far too clumsily for it to be Rupa. He released his hold on the bay and started to turn, his hand drawing his Colt, when something crashed against his shoulder. It was a blow, he knew, that had been aimed at his head, but because he had been in the act of turning around, his assailant had missed his intended target.

He quickly completed his turn and saw the Schofield .45 in the hand of the Tshurara gypsy who was standing not far away from him. As the man raised and fired the gun he had just used to club Cimarron the lawman threw himself to one side. The bullet whistled past Cimarron's head, and he almost fell to the ground, unbalanced from his sudden move. But he quickly recovered and, using his own gun barrel as a club, brought it down upon the gypsy's gun hand.

The gypsy let out a yell; the gun fell from his hand and blood gushed from the spot where Cimarron's gun barrel had broken his skin. Holding his right wrist with his left hand as he hopped about, the man let out another loud cry of pain.

Then, as Cimarron made a grab for him, the Tshurara darted away, still howling at the top of his voice. He'll wake the goddamned dead, Cimarron thought as he sprinted after his quarry, not to mention bring the whole Tshurara tribe down on me if I don't shut the son of a bitch up. When he caught up with the man, he swung the gun in his hand. Its barrel struck and cracked the fleeing gypsy's skull. For a sickening moment, the sound of splintering bone seemed to fill the night and then the man dropped like a stone.

Cimarron hunkered down and pressed two fingers of his left hand against the side of the man's neck. No pulse. He rose and then turned sharply as he heard hurried footsteps behind him, the gun in his hand rising as he swiftly eared back its hammer.

"*Don't!*"

The one word Rupa had spoken from the darkness that

hid her from Cimarron stayed his hand. He sighed and eased the hammer of his .44 back into place.

She gasped as she emerged from the darkness and stood staring down in apparent horror at the gypsy lying on the ground. "He was a Tshurara sentry," she murmured, reaching out to Cimarron, who put an arm around her waist to steady her. "He caught me. He was marching me back to the camp when he heard and then saw you searching for me. He said he would kill me if I didn't lure you toward me so that he could get behind you. Is he dead?"

"As he'll ever be."

"You killed him?"

"Didn't mean to, but I guess I hit him harder than I meant to." Cimarron beckoned to Rupa. "Come on. We've got to get the hell out of here, honey. There's no telling how many more sentries the Tshurara might have posted hereabouts." He asked her where her horse was, and when she told him, he helped her board his bay and then he climbed up behind his saddle's cantle. They moved out at a fast trot.

They had gone no more than a few yards when Cimarron heard the thrashing in the underbrush, warning him that the Tshurara had heard the cries of the sentry and were responding to them. He slammed his heels into his horse's flanks and the animal's pace quickened from a trot to a gallop. When they reached their destination, Rupa dismounted and then boarded her own horse. Cimarron, in the saddle of his bay now, beckoned to her and they galloped away, leaving behind them the angry shouts of the Tshurara gypsies, who were turning the quiet night tumultuous.

They did not speak during the first few miles they traveled side by side, but then, as Cimarron slowed his bay and Rupa matched his pace, she said, "I guess it is time now for us to say good-bye."

"Good-bye?" He gave her a puzzled glance. "How come you're talking about good-bye?"

"Well, I must return to my people and—"

"And I'm going with you."

132

"No! You can't! If you go back to the Lowara, they will kill you!"

"They might try again, but if they do, I'll be ready for them this time."

"Cimarron, you must go away from here, from the Lowara and the Tshurara alike. Both tribes mean you harm."

"I figure I owe Luluvo something for all he did for me when I was blinded. Like how he was ready and willing to take me back to Fort Smith even though he'd not intended traveling in that direction. I've got a warning to give him."

"A warning? About what?"

"Some folks I ran into who are all set to cause you and any other gypsies they can track down a good deal of trouble."

"But, Cimarron, I'm afraid for you. Please, go away. Go back to Fort Smith. Go anywhere. But don't go back to my people; they believe you're a murderer."

"Do you believe I killed Mala?"

"I don't know what to believe. I really don't. I want to believe that you didn't do it. But before Mala died she told Luluvo that her murderer was a lawman who wanted money."

"Come on. Let's get out of here. We're wasting time."

They rode out of the forest minutes later and headed south toward the camp of the Lowara.

Cimarron said nothing when Rupa, riding beside him, remarked, "It is not only the Lowara you have to fear, Cimarron. The Tshurara—Kore and his men—will come hunting for you, and if they find you, they will kill you."

He said nothing in response to her remarks because he felt there was nothing to say. What she had said was true. It was something he would have to deal with when the time came, and he knew it would come—sooner or later.

Cimarron's arrival with Rupa in the Lowara camp at dawn caused an uproar. Men shouted. Women shrieked. Children and dogs, upset by the noise and confusion, began to cry and bark, adding to the din. Someone shouted for Luluvo. Others took up the cry.

He emerged sleeping from his wagon, rubbing his eyes, his hair disheveled. "What—" And then he saw Cimarron, who had dismounted and, with Rupa beside him, was standing stolidly in the center of the camp, seemingly oblivious of the stir his sudden and unexpected appearance had caused.

"Seize him!" Luluvo cried, pointing a stiff finger at Cimarron. "Take him back to the anthill!"

As several of the Lowara men made a move toward him, Cimarron's six-gun cleared leather. "If any of you boys lay a hand on me—or aim a gun at me—there's going to be some dead bodies cluttering up your camp."

"Yours will be one of them," shouted an enraged Luluvo.

"Maybe so," Cimarron stated, "but I'll not be the only man to buy a one-way ticket to hell, old man. Now, what I suggest you all do is simmer down and give a listen to what I've got to say to you."

"Our ears do not want to hear the words of a murderer," a man in the crowd yelled.

"Nor do our eyes want to look upon him," a woman screeched.

Cimarron ignored them both. "After I escaped from the anthill where you put me, I got myself caught by the Tshurara. They took me to their camp."

"Birds of a feather," a man in the crowd muttered darkly. "Troublemakers stick together."

"Now, from what I heard while I was with the Tshurara," Cimarron continued, unperturbed, "those gypsies have been raising Cain in the towns roundabout here. That's probably not news to you, I know. But what may be news to you folks is the fact that there's some Cherokees over in Oaks who are fed up to here with the Tshuraras' thieving and general hell-raising, and those same boys, when I was in Oaks a while back, were doing a dance they call their scalp dance."

"What have the Cherokees to do with us?" Luluvo inquired in a faintly contemptuous tone.

"Plenty," Cimarron promptly responded.

"We should pay no attention to the man who murdered Mala of the Tshurara tribe," a man bellowed. "Lies are on his lips as they were when he spoke before the *kris!*"

"Be silent!" Rupa shot at the man, her eyes blazing. "Let Cimarron speak. Hear him out. He came here to help us. He could have simply gone away. But he didn't. He wanted to—" She fell silent and turned questioning eyes on Cimarron, obviously unsure of exactly why he had returned to the camp with her.

"Those Cherokees I just told you about," Cimarron said when silence had again fallen on the crowd of gypsies, "they have it in mind to do harm to you folks—and to any other gypsies they can lay their hands on. They're all steamed up. They're talking war. And they're talking too about taking scalps."

The silence grew thicker, seeming to smother the gypsies, whose eyes were now all on Cimarron.

Luluvo turned to face Rupa. "What have you to do with this man in whose defense you speak?"

"I couldn't bear to think of him dying in that horrible way," Rupa replied softly, her eyes cast down. "I went to the anthill and I—" She looked up at Luluvo, defiance a bright fire in her black eyes. "I don't care what any of you think of me or what you will say about me. I went there to free Cimarron because I care about him. But I arrived too late. He had already freed himself, but as he has told you, Kore and the men he had with him had taken him prisoner. I followed them back to the Tshurara camp. I helped Cimarron escape from them. We came here. That is all."

"Scandalous," Luluvo snapped angrily. "You should be horsewhipped for behaving like a harlot."

"I'd just like it to be known at this point," Cimarron said in a deceptively mild tone of voice, "that this here lady happens to be a good friend of mine. Now, should any of you set out to do her harm, well, I'd like you to know you'll have me to reckon with if you do."

Luluvo pointed an accusing finger at Rupa, but before he could say anything more, the camp exploded in a cacophony of sound—the pounding of horses' hooves and the firing of guns—as many mounted men rode into it.

As the riders galloped in his direction, Cimarron ducked under the nearest wagon, pulling Rupa to safety with him, his gun still in his hand. The crowd of gypsies scattered and some collided with the galloping horses.

"What—who are they?" Rupa cried in alarm as the men quickly rounded up the fleeing gypsies and disarmed them before any of them could fire so much as a single shot. "What are they doing here?"

Cimarron, from his vantage point on the ground under the wagon, saw a blazing torch materialize in the hand of one of the raiders. He tossed it, a gleeful expression on his face, into one of the wagons, setting it ablaze.

"They're Cherokee Lighthorsemen," he told Rupa in reply to her question. "Don't you recognize the one leading that mob? It's Captain Varnum. He—"

"He was the man who came here with his men the night of the *patshiv*," Rupa breathed. "The one Luluvo paid to leave us alone."

"That's him, all right." Cimarron began to crawl out from under the wagon.

Rupa seized his arm and held him back. "Where are you going?"

"Out there to try to call a halt to Varnum's proceedings."

"Don't leave me, Cimarron!"

He patted her arm reassuringly. "You'll be safe enough under here. You—"

"What if they set this wagon on fire the way they just did that other one?"

"Then you hightail it out from under here and run for the woods. Don't stop running till you're far away from here."

When Rupa nodded, Cimarron eased out from under the wagon, rose, and went racing toward the closest of Varnum's riders. In less than a minute, he had caught up with the man. He ran alongside the Lighthorseman's horse and then made a grab for the man with his free hand. But just as he did so, the man swerved and went galloping off at a right angle to his former path.

Cimarron swore, swerved, and went after him amid the screams of the gypsies and the shouts of the Cherokee Lighthorsemen. The air around him had become smoky from the guns the Indians were still firing into the air.

When Cimarron came up behind his quarry a second time, he wasted no time. He vaulted up over the horse's rump and landed directly behind the cantle of the rider's saddle. He wrapped his left arm around the startled man's neck, his forearm pressing hard against the Indian's windpipe, and then he slid off the horse, taking his prisoner down with him.

The instant they hit the ground, he dragged the Cherokee he had captured behind a wagon. Once there, Cimarron let out a wordless yell at the top of his voice that could be heard above all the other noise in the camp. It had the effect he had wanted it to have, he realized, when he saw Varnum draw rein and turn his horse toward the source of the sound.

"Varnum!" he yelled as he rammed the barrel of his .44 against his prisoner's right temple, "call off your dogs, and call them off right now or I'll blow out the brains of this man I've got an arm on."

Varnum, fury contorting his features, moved his horse in Cimarron's direction, a pistol in his right hand. The men with him closed ranks around him, all of them moving toward Cimarron, who threw his prisoner to the ground and took aim at the obviously frightened man. But his eyes were not on the man lying by his boots, but on Varnum. "Shoot me, Varnum, and your man dies with me."

Varnum drew rein. He held up his hand, and his gesture halted the men riding with him. "What the hell do you think you're doing?"

"That's a question I was just fixing to ask you, Captain. Consider it asked, and consider me waiting for a fast answer from you."

"We're here to clear out this nest of vipers," Varnum

137

declared, his eyes sweeping the campground where some of his men stood guard over the silent gypsies. "We've had complaints from scores of citizens of Cherokee Nation about these people and the larceny they've been practicing on poor hardworking folks. We're here to burn them out. Does that answer your question, Deputy?"

"It sure enough does, Varnum, but at the same time it raises another one in my mind." Cimarron's glance dropped briefly to the man at his feet, and the Lighthorseman, under the harsh glare of those green eyes, froze. Then, looking up at Varnum, Cimarron said, "I seem to recall that these gypsies paid you two hundred dollars in gold to make sure they behaved themselves. A sort of good-faith bond, as I recollect the matter. So, how come you're out here making mischief? They've done no harm to anybody so far as I know."

"No harm?" Varnum repeated, his eyes widening and then narrowing to black slits. "These people have been thieving in Oaks and Salina. Their men seduce our women in both town and country. They have no respect for private property or life. One of them killed that woman of theirs as easily as he'd kill us."

"Nobody's killed any Cherokees that I know of," Cimarron countered. Out of the corner of his eye, he saw his prisoner trying to slither away from him through the dust. He put out a boot and pinned the man to the ground. "Captain, there's something I ought to point out and make plain to you. These gypsies here aren't troublemakers. The ones you want—they're a whole different tribe called the Tshurara—and you can find them camped for the winter just this side of Spavinaw Creek. But let's us get back to the matter of that two hundred dollars I mentioned before. Don't that cut some ice in this matter?"

"I don't know what you're talking about!"

Cimarron's eyebrows arched, his eyes widened, and his lips parted as he assumed an exaggerated expression of surprise.

"You don't, don't you? Then let me freshen your memory some. I was here the night these people—they're

138

called the Lowara, by the way—forked over two hundred dollars in gold to you to leave them be. I saw the money change hands and now you have the nerve to tell me you don't know what I'm talking about when I mention the transaction. You're lying, Varnum. You know about it, all right, and I can prove you do. I've got a whole corral full of witnesses who saw the money change hands that night."

"I never received a red cent from any gypsies," Varnum insisted vehemently.

"There's another thing, Varnum," Cimarron continued. "You signed a paper that night saying you received the money from a man named Luluvo, who's the leader of the Lowara." He turned and called Luluvo's name. When the man appeared from out of a growth of dense underbrush where he had been hiding, he beckoned and Luluvo warily approached him.

"You still got the paper that shows you posted two hundred dollars bond with Captain Varnum here?" he asked, and when Luluvo nodded, he added, "Go get it and show it to the captain."

Luluvo left, and a moment after he had done so, Varnum, who was looking nervously to the right and to the left, suddenly moved his horse forward, shouted a command, and the Lighthorseman Cimarron had downed wriggled out from under Cimarron's boot, leapt to his feet, and went running away.

Cimarron was about to go after him when, in obedience to a command from Varnum, one of the Lighthorsemen fired and his bullet barely missed Cimarron, who drew his gun as Varnum's horse surged toward him. But Varnum kicked the the Colt from his hand while at the same time he shouted an order to his men in the Cherokee language.

The Lighthorseman riding next to Varnum fired unsuccessfully at Luluvo, who was running toward his wagon. As he did so, Cimarron lunged for his gun, retrieved it, and fired a shot that unhorsed the Indian who had tried to hit Luluvo. He fired a second time and his bullet sent Varnum's pistol spinning out of his hand.

"That's enough, Varnum," he bellowed. "Order your men to put up their arms!"

Sullenly, and only after staring hard at Cimarron for a long moment, Varnum gave the order, and the Lighthorsemen all holstered their weapons.

"Step down!" When Varnum hesitated, Cimarron's Colt angled upward until it was aimed directly between the Lighthorse captain's eyes. Varnum got out of the saddle.

"Tell your men to ride on out of here."

Varnum frowned and then reached for his saddle horn, ready to climb aboard his horse again.

"No, not you, Varnum. You're staying right here. Now send your men on their way."

With obvious reluctance, Varnum obeyed Cimarron's order, and when the last of the Lighthorsemen had disappeared, Cimarron yelled, "Luluvo!"

When Luluvo's head appeared from around the rear of his wagon, Cimarron beckoned to him. Moments later, a paper held in his trembling right hand, Luluvo stood beside Cimarron, who took the paper from him and held it out so Varnum could see it.

"This is what you were after the night you snuck into the Lowara camp, wasn't it, Captain?" Cimarron asked in an almost-offhand manner.

Instead of answering, Varnum merely stared at the paper Cimarron was holding out to him. It was the same paper Luluvo had given him to sign the night of the *patshiv* to indicate he had received two hundred dollars in gold as a good faith bond from the Lowara gypsies.

"Luluvo," Cimarron said, his eyes riveted on Varnum, "as I recollect it, you said you found Mala dying outside of your wagon the night somebody attacked her."

"Yes, that is so."

As the gypsies began to gather around the trio, Rupa among them, Cimarron said, "Maybe you folks heard Captain Varnum here tell me a little while ago that he didn't know what I was talking about when I mentioned the two hundred dollars in gold Luluvo had turned over to him."

Murmurs of assent swept through the assemblage of gypsies.

"Maybe you remember something else this Cherokee snake said. He called you thieves"—heads nodded—"and he said you people killed one of your women as easily as you'd kill Cherokees."

Angry voices rumbled about Cimarron. They caused Varnum to shift his stance as if he were looking for a means of escape.

"Now, that last statement of Varnum's, it didn't quite get through to me at the time, but now it makes me wonder about this man." Turning to Varnum, he asked, "Which woman of theirs did these gypsies kill?"

"I—they—I don't know her name."

"How come you know about her being murdered?"

"It was—I heard a rumor about it."

"You're a liar, Varnum!" Cimarron seized a fistful of the Cherokee's shirt and backed him up against one of the wagons. "I'll tell you how you knew a gypsy woman was killed. Because you were the one who murdered her, that's how you knew!"

"No!"

"*Yes!*" Cimarron tightened his grip on Varnum's shirt. "You came here that night to get back the paper—this piece of paper"—he shook it in Varnum's face—"so that there'd be no proof that you ever got two hundred dollars from these gypsies. You wanted that money for yourself."

Varnum started to say something but Cimarron slammed him back against the wagon, cutting off his words. "Hear me out! You snuck into camp. Mala must have come upon you either before or after you got into Luluvo's wagon. She told me once that she had heard about you and about the gold that had been paid over to you. The way I figure it now, she must have asked you what you were doing prowling around the camp and you told her, and then you hit her with the hammer you took from Luluvo's wagon."

Varnum shook his head vigorously in denial of Cimarron's charge.

"When Luluvo found and questioned Mala later as she

lay dying, she was only able to tell him that it was a lawman, who was after money, who had attacked her."

"That's crazy," Varnum protested, sweat beginning to stream down his face. "That's about the craziest story I ever heard concocted in all my life."

"You ordered one of your men to shoot Luluvo just now when I sent him to fetch this here paper." Cimarron again thrust it in front of Varnum's face. "You figured to keep him from getting it—"

"He was running away. My man fired a warning shot at him."

"Like hell he did! He shot to kill. It's a damned good thing your man is no marksman. The way I see it, you figured that if you could put Luluvo out of the way, you'd have another crack at getting your hands on this paper. And once you had it, you knew there was no way for anybody to prove beyond a reasonable doubt that these gypsies had paid you so much as a red cent, never mind two hundred dollars." Cimarron let go of Varnum and stepped back. He drew his gun. "I want to hear the truth from you, Varnum. If I don't hear it, I just might kill you—slow. I'll start by shooting off your ears." He cocked his gun.

"No! Don't!"

Cimarron fired, deliberately missing Varnum, his bullet tearing through the canvas wall of the wagon behind the Indian.

"I'll pay back the money. Every dime of it!" Varnum wailed.

Cimarron again eared back the hammer of his .44.

"All right!" Varnum screeched, his eyes bulging. "I did it. But it was an accident. It happened like you said. I came here looking for that paper I'd signed—you were right about that. The woman caught me at it. She guessed what I was after and she wanted a cut of the two hundred to keep quiet."

"And you weren't willing to give it to her?" Cimarron prompted when Varnum fell silent.

The Lighthorseman nodded with obvious reluctance. "I

hit her with a hammer I found in the old man's wagon. I didn't mean to kill her, but she made me mad. She was standing there taunting me, saying she'd tell on me and the gypsies would cut off my balls, things like that. I had to do it. She gave me no choice!"

Cimarron spat in disgust. Then, keeping his gun trained on Varnum, he took a pair of handcuffs from his saddlebag. He barked an order, and when Varnum had wrapped his arms around a birch tree's trunk and pressed his back up against it, the lawman snapped the handcuffs on Varnum's wrist.

Cimarron turned as a heavy hand fell on his forearm, to find Luluvo standing beside him.

"My heart is heavy," Luluvo declared in a cracked voice. "I and the other *krisatora*—the entire Lowara tribe—we have all done you a grave injustice. And the rashness of our act could have cost you your life. I must most humbly ask your forgiveness, Cimarron, on behalf of all of us."

As Luluvo lowered his head, unable to meet Cimarron's eyes, Cimarron reached out and clapped a hand on the old man's shoulder. "Things just aren't always what they seem, Luluvo. What Mala told you about her murderer did make it look to you like I was the one who killed her. I'm just glad I finally figured out what really happened that night."

Luluvo looked up at him. "I too am glad. But I am also ashamed of what we did to you."

"All that's water under the dam, Luluvo. Let's forget it. You've got other more important things to concern you now."

"What things?" Luluvo asked easily.

"Those Cherokee scalp-hunters I told you about before. You'd best get to pulling up stakes before they show up here looking for some gypsy hair to lift."

9

"But we have caused the *gaje* no trouble," Luluvo stated with a plaintive note in his voice. "So we are not the ones the Indians will attack. They will attack the Tshurara, who have caused them trouble."

As he thumbed cartridges out of his gun belt and into the empty chambers of his Colt's cylinder, Cimarron shook his head. "Those scalp-hunters won't be asking who belongs to what tribe when they go on the warpath. To them, one gypsy looks like every other gypsy. They'll harm any one of you they chance upon, mark my words, Luluvo."

The old man's shoulders slumped as Cimarron holstered his gun. "Then we must flee as you advise." He sighed. "It is the same story all the time. The *gaje* hate us, so they hunt us and we must always run from them. From place to place. From country to country. We Rom have never known peace, nor will we ever know any, I fear."

"Were I you, Luluvo," Cimarron said, spinning the cylinder of his gun until the chamber he had deliberately left empty was beneath its hammer, "I'd stay off the roads and any well-traveled trails. I'd keep out of sight as much as possible. Take some of the straw you've been using for fodder and pad your horses' hooves with it. You can bind the straw in place with rope or pieces of cloth. That way

your caravan'll make little noise and you won't make yourselves any more noticeable than necessary."

Luluvo nodded and they frowned as Rupa joined them.
"Child," he said, "I wronged you earlier with my hasty
words."

Rupa smiled. "Your temper and tongue are quick, Luluvo.
They can trip you."

He gave her a rueful smile. "Then you forgive me?"

"How can I forgive you?"

Luluvo's face fell.

"When I have forgotten what there is to forgive?" Rupa
added.

"I will alert the camp—tell them that we must leave
here," Luluvo declared with sudden animation. Addressing Cimarron, he asked, "Will you ride at the head or the
rear of the caravan?"

"Neither one," Cimarron answered.

"I don't understand."

"Luluvo, Kore and his boys are likely to be out hunting
my hide. Were I to travel along with you, I'd be like a
lightning rod drawing them right to you. I could be the
cause of some of your people getting hurt or maybe even
killed, should Kore come looking for me in your caravan,
which seems to me like a thing he just might do."

"If Kore comes, we will fight together, Cimarron. You
and the Rom shall stand shoulder to shoulder. We have
guns. Our men are brave."

"But not foolhardy, Luluvo. Nope, I reckon it's best I
leave you now and head on back to Fort Smith."

"Perhaps you are right," Luluvo admitted. "But please,
don't leave us yet. I will tell everyone to get ready to
break camp and then I will return to you. Wait for me,
Cimarron. Will you do that?"

Cimarron hesitated a moment, but then, catching the
eager look Rupa gave him, he said, "I'll wait for you,
Luluvo. Only hurry on back, hear? The sooner you folks
get as far away from here as you can, the better off you'll
all be."

When Luluvo had gone, Rupa looked up at Cimarron and, with a sigh, murmured. "*Vadni rasta.*"

"Beg pardon, honey? What's that you said?"

"Wild goose," Rupa replied. "That's what you are. You go where you please when you please. Nothing and no one can hold you."

"I'm a lot like you gypsies in that respect, I reckon."

"But the Rom travel with one another. We are together. You are alone."

"That's true enough."

"You do not want to stay with me?"

"Now, honey, don't you go stuffing my mouth full of your words. I didn't say that. What I told Luluvo was—"

Rupa suddenly whirled away from Cimarron, her skirts swirling about her trim ankles, and strode into the middle of the camp where the Lowara were busily packing their belongings, striking their tents, binding their horses' hooves with straw as Cimarron had suggested to Luluvo, and filling their water barrels for the journey facing them.

When Rupa had vanished in the crowd, Cimarron led his bay to the wagon he had been using and tethered it to a nearby tree. He climbed into the wagon and lay down on his tick, his hands clasped behind his head as he listened to the sounds of the Lowara as they prepared to break camp, and he wondered why Luluvo had asked him to wait.

He yawned and then closed his eyes. Minutes later he was asleep.

He was drifting in a dream in which he saw himself the warden of a prison that had silk instead of stone walls and velvet instead of iron bars. Absolute lord of his domain, he was reveling in the startling beauty of his prisoners—all of whom were women and none of whom ever rejected his eager advances—when he suddenly snapped awake at the sound of a creaking board.

He blinked and reached out to seize the shadowy form bending over him while at the same time thrusting aside the intruder's raised right hand, which held a long knife.

The figure eluded him and scurried away. He leapt to

his feet and lunged, bringing the intruder down and only then did he realize that his prisoner was a naked woman whose features were hidden by her long black hair.

He forced her to drop her knife, and then, as her head rose and she looked directly at him, a woebegone expression marring her attractive face, he exclaimed, "*Rupa!*"

She began to cry, covering her face with her free hand, and turned away from him.

"What's this all about, honey?" he asked, stunned to find her in his wagon and more stunned still to find her there without clothes.

"I recited the spell," she sobbed. "Then I took off my clothes in the woods and came into your wagon."

"With a knife? Why?"

"It is gypsy sorcery," she whimpered.

"What is?"

"The spell—the enchantment. A woman goes naked to the man she loves, careful not to be seen by anyone. But I failed!"

As Rupa sobbed disconsolately, both hands covering her face, her shoulders shaking, Cimarron, aroused by the erotic sight of her voluptuous body, put his arms around her and drew her close to him.

"Take it easy, honey. Whatever it is that's troubling you, it'll pass. Don't cry."

"It won't!" Rupa cried, and let out an anguished wail. "I wasn't going to hurt you with that." She pointed to the knife lying at her feet. "I was just going to cut a lock of your hair. To make the sorcery work, a woman must first recite the proper spell. I did that. Then she must come naked to the place where her beloved lies sleeping and she must take care to be seen by no one. I did that too, and that part was very difficult because it seems that everyone in camp is moving about. But I couldn't wait for the cover of darkness, when it would have been easier. You might have gone away before then."

She sniffed and wiped the tears from her eyes with the backs of her hand. "I was just about to cut a lock of your hair when you awoke and found me here.

"Now—now that you have caught me before I could finish—the enchantment will all go the other way, and I am as bad off now as I was before I tried to cast the spell upon you. Worse off!" Rupa let out another heartful wail.

Cimarron, as he stroked her shoulder, her back, the rounded curve of her buttocks, felt himself stiffening. "I don't follow you, honey. What do you mean you're worse off now than you were before?"

"If the woman is caught by the man she loves as she tries to cut a lock of his hair, she will fail to make him fall in love with her. Instead, she will become hopelessly in love with him!"

"Rupa, you don't need any spells or enchantments or any of that kind of stuff to make me like you. I—"

"Like!" she echoed, and burst into tears again. "I don't want you to like me! I want you to love me!"

Cimarron's eyes rolled heavenward as he continued to caress Rupa. He shifted his body so that his erection was pressing stiffly against her loins. "I sure do wish you wouldn't cry. It makes me about as skittish as a green bronc at the touch of the first saddle he's ever felt."

She stopped crying. She looked up into his eyes. Hopefully.

He caressed her cheek and then bent and kissed her lips. "You've got real soft skin. Dark like it is, it makes me think of brown satin."

"You do not like me because I am not white like the women of the gaje?"

"I like you fine just the way you are." Cimarron kissed her again, and then, thrusting his tongue into her mouth, he began to explore it.

When their lips parted, Rupa, her eyes twinkling, whispered, "May kali i muri may gugli avela. That means, 'The darker the berry, the sweeter it is.'" As she sank down upon the tick lying on the floor of the wagon, she pulled Cimarron beside her.

Then, like a woman gone wild, she began to tear at his clothes, her hands frantic as she, with his eager help, quickly stripped them from his body. When he was as naked as she was, Rupa nearly attacked him, and he not only welcomed but willingly submitted to her erotic assault. She tumbled about on the tick, her hands groping, her mouth searching, and he, smelling the musk of her arousal, returned her attentions even more amorously until their intertwined bodies, a wild tangle of arms and legs, seemed to have become melded together and incapable of ever again separating.

Before he could plunge into her, she was above him and bending down. Kneeling between his spread legs, she took him in her mouth. His neck arched and his head bent backward as ecstasy began to ripple through every cell in his body. Rupa's head bobbed up and down and her hot tongue laved his rigid shaft, while he took her breasts in his hands and then, to prevent himself from erupting before she climaxed, he pulled out of her mouth and drew her toward him. He raised his head and began to suck her right breast, teasing her nipple with his tongue until it stiffened and she moaned with wordless pleasure.

"I want you!" she cried. She pushed him aside, lay down on her back, and clawed at him until he was on top of her.

He probed and then entered her, supporting himself on his hands, his torso angled upward as he looked down at her where she lay beneath him, her eyes closed, her arms flung out, and sweat streaking her face as she tossed her head from side to side. He eased down until he was lying on top of her. His hips rose and fell, rose and fell. He felt the pressure mounting within him and then a momentary sensation akin to light-headedness.

Rupa cried out and shuddered under him. She gripped his arms, and her legs wound themselves around his waist. She thrust upward, her back arched, and he knew she had found release. He plunged into her as far as he could go, and she groaned as he did so. As he continued to buck, he felt the familiar force building within him, and when he erupted a moment later, he gripped Rupa's shoulders and uttered a long, drawn-out sigh of intense pleasure.

They lay there then, both of them sated and spent, until finally Rupa whispered, "Now you understand."

"I do?"

"About the sorcery. I am the one, because of my failure to clip your hair and escape unseen by you, who is enchanted. Enslaved. Bound to you by the chains of love."

"I'm not exactly what you could call disinterested in you either, honey," he told her sincerely. "You saw how it was with me just now."

Rupa gently caressed his cheek. "You are a good lover. Sweet but fiery. A man who knows how to please a woman and yet leave her wanting you all the more afterward."

Still within her, Cimarron swiveled his hips slightly.

Rupa sighed and clutched him to her.

Still stiff, he began to move again, slowly at first and then more rapidly. When he felt her stir and begin to match his rhythm and its increasing tempo, he nuzzled her neck. Slipping his hands beneath her buttocks, he pressed her against him. Suddenly, he withdrew from her, and when her eyes snapped open in surprise, he reentered her, this time almost savagely. But despite the strength and depth of his abrupt thrust, Rupa softly sighed with pleasure.

Twice more he brought her to a climax, and then he let himself explode, feeling an overwhelming and thoroughly satisfying sense of release as his hips continued to lurch and the last of the hot lava flowed from his body into Rupa's.

Finally, he withdrew from her and lay down beside her. As he gently caressed her breasts and the lovely hills and valleys on the landscape of her lush body, he murmured, "Maybe you'd better give some thought to how you're going to get out of here without being seen."

"You want to get rid of me," she said petulantly.

"Nope. I could stay like this forever and a day. But we've got to be practical."

"I left my clothes in the woods at the foot of a deadfall not far from the wagon. Would you get them for me?"

Cimarron got up and proceeded to dress. He left the

wagon and returned less than five minutes later with Rupa's clothes. He sat on the tick and watched her dress, admiring her graceful movements and the play of light and shadow on her voluptuous body.

She reached out, drew him to his feet, and kissed him passionately. "Will you watch for me? Tell me when it is safe to leave?"

He did, and minutes later she climbed down from the wagon and fled like a hunted fawn into the forest.

He sighed and closed his eyes. An afterimage of Rupa burned brightly in the darkness behind his closed eyelids. As she, in his mind's eye, undulated seductively and eagerly beckoned to him, he felt himself becoming rigid again. To banish the image and the desire it was stirring within him, he opened his eyes and went in search of Luluvo.

He found the old man on the far side of the camp and he told him that he was leaving.

"I have been so busy," the leader of the Lowara declared, clearly flustered. "But I didn't forget about you, Cimarron. And now that we are all ready to leave here, it is time."

"Time? Time for what?"

Instead of answering, Luluvo shouted and then beckoned to the gypsies. When all of them had gathered about him and Cimarron, he announced, "This *gajo* saved us from the Lighthorsemen led by the infamous Captain Varnum who were bent on killing us. We owe our lives to him. Is it not so?"

Cimarron heard the shouts in the Romany language and he judged by the nodding heads of the gypsies that they had agreed with Luluvo.

"No money can pay for what you did for us, Cimarron," Luluvo continued. "But no *gajo* such as yourself can truly share the life of the Lowara. Only those of our blood can do that. Therefore, you will become our brother."

Before Cimarron could react, Luluvo turned from him, and when he turned back, he held in his hand a sharp dagger that had been given to him by one of the men in the surrounding crowd. He ordered Cimarron to bare his right arm, and when Cimarron had willingly done so, he used the point of the dagger to make an incision in Cimarron's forearm just above his wrist. As the blood began to flow from the cut, Luluvo did the same to his own right forearm and then pressed the two bleeding wounds together.

"Let our blood mix," he intoned solemnly, and a moment later withdrew his arm from Cimarron's. He gestured and a man stepped out of the crowd. Luluvo incised the man's forearm after which the man placed it against Cimarron's bleeding forearm.

The process was repeated until all the men in the tribe had blended their blood with Cimarron's.

Luluvo then formally announced that the Lowara tribe now had a new member. "Now will I give our blood brother his gypsy name!" he declared. "Zurka!" he cried, pointing at Cimarron.

"Zurka!" echoed all the gypsies at the tops of their voices.

Luluvo, addressing Cimarron, asked him to swear that he would, when with the gypsies, live by their tribal laws.

Cimarron swore as the blood on his wrist began to clot.

Luluvo handed him the dagger and whispered instructions to him.

Obeying Luluvo's instructions, Cimarron first touched the point of the bloody blade to Luluvo's chest and then made his way through the crowd, touching the chest of each of his blood brothers with the dagger's tip. When he returned, he handed the blade to Luluvo, who gave it back to its owner. Then he submitted to Luluvo's bearlike embrace as more cheers erupted from the throats of the watching gypsies.

Cimarron held out his hand when Luluvo released him, and Luluvo took it in a firm grip and shook it.

"You go now?" he asked. Cimarron nodded. "I'll be taking Captain Varnum back with me to Fort Smith. But first I want to see how much money he's carrying, since he owes you two hundred dollars."

Cimarron left Luluvo and went over to the tree to which he had handcuffed Varnum. "Captain, I reckon you won't mind if I go through your pockets."

"I damn well will and do mind," Varnum roared. He cursed as Cimarron thrust a hand into one of his prisoner's pockets.

Moments later, Cimarron commented, "Not much of a haul, but it'll do till the court sees to it that you make restitution to these gypsies for the money you owe them."

Varnum continued swearing as Cimarron left him and rejoined Luluvo, to whom he handed the twenty-one dollars and four cents he had taken from Varnum's pockets. Then, after shaking hands once more, he left Luluvo, retrieved his bay, and returned to Varnum. He unlocked the man's handcuffs, and then, leading his horse, he marched his prisoner in the direction of Varnum's horse, which stood idly grazing near the rope corral that contained the gypsies' extra stock.

But before he reached it, he was ambushed by Varnum's Cherokee Lighthorsemen, who erupted like apparitions from the bushes on his right. They had apparently been hiding and waiting for an opportunity to free their leader. He had no time to draw his gun, nor did he have time to defend himself as several men quickly seized him and dragged him quietly into the bushes. One of them struck him twice on the head with a gun barrel and sent him spinning swiftly into senselessness.

Consciousness returned to Cimarron like a thief in the night. Stealthily. Tentatively.

He opened his eyes, blinked, and then closed them again as if, by so doing, he could banish the pain that racketed through his skull where the gun barrel of one of Varnum's Cherokee Lighthorsemen had landed—how long ago? He opened his eyes again and sat up. He looked up at the sky; at first, it was nothing but a gold-and-blue blur. Then, as the pain in his head diminished slightly, the sky and the sun slowly came into focus. It's well past noon, he thought as he noted the position of the sun. I've been out for hours.

He picked up his hat, which had fallen from his head when he had been struck, and put it on. He got slowly to his feet, not daring to move more than was necessary in order to prevent more pain than what he was already experiencing. He leaned for a moment against the trunk of a tree, and then, moving slowly, he made his way out of the dense undergrowth.

When he reached the camp, he found it deserted. Nothing remained of it but the cold ashes of cooking fires, traces of ruts left in the ground by wagon wheels, and a yellow kerchief that someone had either lost or abandoned. The gypsies, he thought, must have figured I'd ridden out. Me and Varnum.

He made his way to where his bay was browsing on a chokecherry bush, climbed into the saddle, and set out to trail Varnum and his Lighthorsemen. Keeping his eyes on the tracks made by the hooves of his quarry's horses, he heeled his bay into a canter.

But, moments later, when he heard the sound of horses off to his left, he drew rein and his hand hit the butt of his Colt. Turning his horse into the cover of some shin oaks, he unleathered his gun, ready this time for the Lighthorsemen he believed had returned to finish him off.

But when the first of the riders came into sight in the north, he saw that they were not Varnum's men, but Kore and his riders. Eleven of them, he counted. Not such hot odds were I try to go up against that gang.

"The Lowara are gone, Kore," one of the Tshurara yelled.

"I've got eyes," Kore yelled back, an expression of fury on his face. "I can see that they're gone." He pointed to the wheel-rutted ground. "They're heading south. Let's go get that lawman they've got with them."

As Kore and his men rode away from the deserted campsite, Cimarron sat his saddle for a moment and then, abandoning his plan to trail Varnum, rode out of the trees and headed west, intending to try to overtake and then bypass Kore and his men so that he could warn the Lowara that trouble was traveling their backtrail.

If Kore catches up with them and finds I'm not there, he thought as he urged his bay into a gallop, there's no telling what that evil son of a bitch might do to Luluvo and his people out of pure down-and-out meanness.

He rode for nearly a mile, lashing his bay with his reins, and then turned south, beginning to travel a trail that ran parallel to the one taken by Kore and his men. He knew he had to outdistance the Tshurara and he also knew that the Lowara could be many long miles ahead of him. Already his horse was beginning to sweat, and before he had gone another mile, strings of white lather were torn from the animal's body by the onrushing wind into which horse and rider were heading.

This wind is slowing me down, he thought. He peered at the landscape ahead of him through slitted eyes, and when he spotted a series of rolling hummocks ahead of him, he made for them. As he rode up and then topped the tallest of them, he gazed east and then south. But it was not until he turned his gaze north that he spotted the clouds of dust raised by distant riders. That's them, he thought exultantly. He galloped down the hummock and rode hard across a grassy expanse of ground. He hoped that little or no dust would rise to betray his presence on the plain. He glanced back over his shoulder from time to time as he rode. No sign of Kore. Good. He slammed his heels into his horse's flanks and the animal galloped on gamely.

Minutes later, the grassy plain abruptly gave way to a broad expanse of rocky ground littered with frost-cracked shale that had fallen from tall outcroppings of rock. He was just about to veer to the left toward smoother terrain when his horse suddenly threw a shoe and broke stride. Immediately, the animal's gait altered, becoming ungainly. It slowed its pace as it began to favor its right shoeless front hoof.

Cimarron swore aloud. He drew rein, bringing the bay

to a trot and then to a walk. He halted the animal and dismounted, knowing he had no choice but to do so if he didn't want to injure the animal's unshod hoof. Leaving his mount ground hitched, he walked back the way he had come, and finally, after careful searching, he found the lost shoe. He picked it up, returned to his bay, and placed the shoe in his saddlebag. Then, picking up the reins, he began to lead the horse in a southerly direction.

As he walked, the sun gradually dipped lower in the sky, and by the time the haphazard cluster of Lowara wagons came into sight on the southern horizon, it was low in the western sky. He halted and surveyed the distant scene. No sign of Kore and his men. The Lowara did not seem to be in the process of setting up a camp for the night. Those he could see from his vantage point were merely milling about in an apparently aimless fashion.

He resumed his journey, and as he neared the wagons, he moved cautiously, his keen green eyes watching for sign of something out of the ordinary, his equally keen ears listening for any sound that might spell danger. He stopped when he was still some distance away from the wagons, and standing as still as a stone, he studied the gypsies and the surrounding area. When he saw nothing amiss, he moved on and minutes later he rejoined the Lowara.

He was greeted with a babble of voices speaking the Romany language. He interrupted them by speaking a single word—a name: "Luluvo."

Someone brought him to the old man, who looked badly shaken—even sick, Cimarron thought.

"Cimarron! What are you doing here?"

Noting that Luluvo's voice seemed lifeless, he quickly summarized what had happened to him just before the Lowara left their camp earlier in the day. "I came to warn you folks that Kore and his hardcases are out stalking you folks, Luluvo. They—"

"I know. They were here."

Cimarron gritted his teeth. A muscle in his jaw jumped. So he was too late!

"They wanted you, Cimarron," Luluvo declared, still speaking in that disturbingly lifeless tone that was so uncharacteristic of him. "I told them you were not here. I told them that you had taken Captain Varnum and ridden east on your way back to Fort Smith. That was what I believed you had done when you disappeared from our camp earlier today. But Kore called me a liar. He said he saw Captain Varnum and his men at a makeshift camp north of Locust Grove when he was on his way to us. He said I was lying to keep him from finding you. He was convinced we were hiding you from him."

Luluvo paused, swallowed hard, and then continued, "He and his men searched our wagons in an attempt to find you. Rupa, unfortunately, taunted them. She said that even if they should capture you again, she would come and free you as she did before. When Kore heard that, he slapped her face so hard he sent her sprawling."

"I'll kill the bastard for that," Cimarron snarled. Then, "Is she all right? Where is Rupa? I'd like to see her and—"

Luluvo shook his head. "She is gone."

"Gone? Gone where?"

"Kore took her," Luluvo answered. "When Rupa boldly told him that she—that she had a great deal of feeling for you—he decided to take her with him."

"Why'd he do that?"

"Kore is a clever and dangerous man. He reasoned, based on what I had told him and what he had seen, that Captain Varnum had escaped from you. He said he believed you would probably rejoin us since you obviously no longer had a prisoner. He said you would do so to help protect us from him. He said you were the kind of man who could be expected to do such a thing since, he said, you were an honorable, as well as a foolish, man."

"I'll go after him," Cimarron vowed. "I'll get Rupa away from him."

"That is exactly why he took her, he told us," Luluvo stated sadly. "He is using her to lure you to him since he did not know where you could be found, nor did we."

"Him and me, then, we're both in the same boat. I don't know where he can be found."

"I can tell you that. Kore told us he and his men would camp on Icy Creek. They would wait for you there. And while they waited, he said"—Luluvo lowered his head—"he would force Rupa to—to entertain them."

"I need a horse, Luluvo. Mine threw a shoe."

"You are going to Icy Creek?"

"I am. And I'm going to kill Kore if that's what it takes to get Rupa away from him and those other animals siding him."

"The Lowara men—we will go with you."

Cimarron shook his head. "I don't want you folks hurt. I'll go alone." Then he held up his hand to silence Luluvo's protest.

The old gypsy took in Cimarron's grim look, his rigid posture, and knew that it would do no good to argue.

He had a horse—a chestnut—brought, and Cimarron quickly transferred his gear to it. He removed his bay's thrown shoe from his saddlebag and handed it to Luluvo. "I'd be obliged to you if you could get someone to nail this back on," he said, mounting the chestnut.

"Yayal will do it," Luluvo promised. "He is a good blacksmith as well as an excellent horse trader." For the first time, Luluvo managed a smile. Remembering Yayal and how he had deceived the *gajo* at the horse-trading fair into believing the nag he was selling was young and spirited, Cimarron also smiled.

But seconds later, while riding toward Icy Creek, Cimarron was grim. He was thinking of Rupa and what she might be suffering at the hands of Kore and his riders.

10

Cimarron sat below the crest of the hill from which he had spotted the crude camp Kore and his men had made on the bank of Icy Creek. He forcibly emptied his mind of thoughts of Rupa and what might be happening to her in the camp as he waited for the sun to set.

Later, when darkness had claimed the land, he rose and, leaving his borrowed chestnut ground hitched behind him, crested the hill and then made his way down it, moving swiftly, secure in the knowledge that he could not be seen against the background of the night-blackened hill. When he neared the camp, he circled it silently, searching for a suitable spot from which he could reconnoiter the area before moving out on his mission to rescue Rupa. He chose a spot between a low boulder and a towering loblolly pine that grew next to it. He squeezed himself into a space between the tree and the boulder and surveyed the camp lighted by the flames of a low-burning campfire.

Men sat around it, drinking coffee from tin cans that had once held tomatoes. Kore was not among them. But then, as Cimarron continued watching, Kore emerged from the bushes, dragging Rupa behind him. Cimarron's teeth ground together at the sight of her dirt-streaked face and torn blouse.

"Who's next?" the Tshurara leader called out cheerfully, and when a gypsy sitting by the fire shot to his feet, he shoved Rupa in the man's direction.

Kore's grinning confederate seized Rupa by the right wrist and began to drag her back into the bushes. She fought him valiantly with her free hand and both feet, but in vain. They vanished.

Cimarron rose, eased out from between the tree and boulder, and pulled his bowie knife from his boot. He circled the camp, moving stealthily and without noise, as he made his way toward the bushes that now sheltered Rupa and the man with her. As he came closer to them, he heard the sound of tearing cloth and Rupa's whimpering. Then, as he came still closer to them, he was able to see the two figures in the dim light of the moon. His back to Cimarron, the man was straddling Rupa, who lay on her back, her wrists pinned to the ground. His trousers halfway down around his hairy thighs, he probed her with his stiff shaft.

Cimarron moved closer to him, his bowie knife in his right hand. When he was only two feet from the rutting man, his left arm suddenly shot out and his forearm snapped back against the man's throat. He pulled him off Rupa, who let out a startled gasp and sprang to her feet.

The gypsy Cimarron had by the throat gagged and then suddenly twisted his body violently and tore free of Cimarron. "Kore!" he screamed.

The laughter of the men around the campfire in the distance stopped and someone called out, "What's the matter, Pulika? You need some help with the little lady?"

"Don't!" Pulika pleaded as he tried to pull up his trousers with one hand and ward off the knife in Cimarron's hand with the other. "Don't cut me! You want her, take her. She's yours. Go ahead, have at her if you want her."

"Come on, Rupa," Cimarron said. "We're getting out of here. Mister, you're coming with us, and you're coming nice and quiet. If I hear so much as another peep out of you, I'll gut you. You got that?"

Pulika nodded, his eyes wide with fear. "Which way?"

Cimarron pointed with the knife in his hand, and the man, after managing to pull up his trousers and belt them, moved out in the direction Cimarron had indicated.

"You saw?" Rupa asked Cimarron as he took her hand and began to trail Pulika. When he said nothing, she repeated, "You saw." But this time it was a despairing statement, not a hesitant question.

"You've got nothing to be ashamed of, Rupa," he told her in a tight voice. "What happened wasn't your fault."

"But it happened," she snarled, her voice vicious. "Four of them took me. One of them even made me—" Her voice abruptly died. Suddenly, she turned on Cimarron and ripped the knife from his hand.

Before he could make the slightest move to retrieve it, she was racing away from him toward the Tshurara gypsy just ahead of them. She halted when she reached Pulika, who, hearing her approach, turned startled eyes upon her. Holding Cimarron's bowie knife in both of her hands, Rupa swiftly raised it high above her head and then as swiftly brought it down.

Its blade pierced Pulika's chest, driving deep into its fleshy target. Not content with what she had done, Rupa savagely twisted the blade, first one way and then the other.

Pulika made an aborted series of gargling sounds, his hands clutching frantically at the knife, as he attempted but failed to pull it free of his chest. His knees began to buckle and then they gave way. Blood gushed from his wide-open mouth, through which he was desperately trying to swallow air as he went down and his bulging eyes began to glaze.

Cimarron, who had come up behind Rupa only an instant after she had dealt Pulika the fatal blow, bent down and pulled his knife from the dead man's body. He wiped its blade on some grass and then booted it.

"Let's go!" he said tersely. He took Rupa's trembling hand and together they ran to where he had left his horse. When they reached it, they both boarded it. Then, as Rupa wrapped her arms around his waist and pressed her cheek against his broad back from where she sat behind the cantle of his saddle, Cimarron slammed his heels into the chestnut's flanks and they went galloping away from Kore's camp.

"What's that?" Rupa asked nervously. Cimarron listened to the sound of firing that could be heard in the distance as they neared the spot where he had last seen the Lowara.

"Don't know for sure. But I reckon it means trouble." He drew rein and slid out of the saddle. "You stay up there," he told Rupa, and then moved cautiously forward through the forest that surrounded them. "Shit!" he muttered a moment later when he caught sight of the mounted men who were attacking the gypsies. That goddamned Capt. Varnum, he thought angrily, he's like a bad penny a man just can't get shut of. He just keeps on turning up.

He drew his .44 as the gypsies struggled desperately to circle their wagons to give themselves some measure of protection from the withering fire of Captain Varnum and the other attacking Cherokee Lighthorsemen.

I can't take that whole mob of marauders, he thought. His finger tightened on his trigger. But I can take Varnum. He raised his gun, took careful aim, and shot Varnum's horse in the head. Then, as Varnum went flying over his horse's head and the animal hit the ground hard, Cimarron ran out of the forest and directly into the middle of the melee.

Like an arrow fired with deadly and accurate aim, he headed for his target: Varnum. He dodged horses and a man on foot as he zigzagged through clouds of gunsmoke on his way toward his quarry, narrowly escaping a trampling by a big black gelding ridden by a slit-eyed and sweating Cherokee.

When he reached Varnum, he pounced on him like a giant cat that had successfully stalked and trapped a canary. Hauling the man to his feet, he half-carried and half-dragged Varnum through a gap in the wagons and into the midst of the Lowara gypsies, who were firing back at the Indians to little avail.

"Cimarron!"

He caught a glimpse of Luluvo in the distance, and then, as the leader of the Lowara hurried toward him, he thrust the muzzle of his six-gun up against Varnum's Adam's apple. "Don't you move a muscle," he commanded. "You do, and I'll blow your brains away."

Varnum stood rigidly, his eyes cast down and seemingly glued to Cimarron's gun, the barrel of which was less than an inch below his quivering chin.

"They wanted you," Luluvo blurted out as he came running up to Cimarron. "They wouldn't believe me when I told them you weren't here. They—"

Cimarron, out of the corner of his eye, saw a Lighthorseman ride up on the far side of the wagons and take fast aim with a Winchester .44 carbine. His left arm shot out, knocking Luluvo to the ground. But he had made his move seconds too late. He stared down in dismay at the blood blossoming in the V formed by the neckline of Luluvo's open shirt. Then, spinning around, he got off a snap shot, and the Cherokee who had just wounded Luluvo threw up his arms, dropped his gun, and fell from his horse. Cimarron fired a second time before the man had even hit the ground, and this time his shot hit his target's skull, opening up a bloody valley of torn flesh and broken bone.

Gripping Varnum's collar in his left hand, he forced the man to climb up on the tongue of the nearest wagon. When Varnum had done so, Cimarron climbed up behind him and muttered an order in the Lighthorseman's ear.

"Cease firing!" Varnum cried in obedience to Cimarron's command, wildly waving his arms. "*Cease firing!*"

His men obeyed him. When there was silence in the area, Cimarron spoke to the Indian lawmen who were milling about on their horses and on foot, their eyes shifting from him to Varnum and back to him again. "This man tried to steal two hundred dollars from the people he talked you into attacking twice. Now, I happen to be a lawman, same as you." He dug his badge out of his pocket and held it up for the Cherokees to see. "In my reading of the law, what Varnum did's larceny, and I'm going to see to it that he stands trial for his crime before Judge Parker in Fort Smith.

"I'd advise you boys, if you don't want to see Varnum get hurt, to back off same as you did last time. If you don't, I might have to shoot your captain. It don't make all that much difference to me how it's to be for him. A trial in Fort Smith—or my bullet in his gut. It's all up to you fellows. So take your choice."

The Indians milling about muttered among themselves for several minutes, during which Varnum frantically pleaded with them to do what Cimarron had advised.

"He's a bloodthirsty beast," Varnum shrieked. "So back off for my sake!"

Cimarron didn't relax until the last of the Lighthorsemen had turned his mount and started to ride away. "Glad to see how smart you boys are," he called out tauntingly to them. "If you'd have stayed, I'd have fought you till hell froze over and we could all skate on the ice."

Ignoring the furious glances the Indians threw over their shoulders at him, he continued, "Should any of you fellows take a notion to come back a third time—well, don't do it. If you do, I'll have to catch each and every one of you on account of you're all accessories after the fact in your captain's crime. And should you happen to get away from me—well, I've got keen eyes and have been known to track a bear through running water."

He suppressed a smile as he stood on the wagon tongue with the trembling Varnum and watched the Lighthorsemen disappear into the forest.

When they were gone, he turned to a gypsy standing near him. "Rupa's over there in the woods." He pointed to the spot where he had left her. "I'd be obliged to you if you'd go get her and fetch her back here."

As the gypsy headed for the woods, Cimarron ordered Varnum to sit down on the ground, and when the

Lighthorseman had done so, he handcuffed him to a tree some distance away from the gypsies' wagons.

Then he made his way back to the spot where Luluvo lay on the ground surrounded by members of his tribe. He shouldered his way through the subdued crowd and hunkered down next to the old man and the even older woman who was swabbing the bullet wound in the base of Luluvo's throat with a bloody piece of wet muslin.

"We'll put you in your wagon," he told Luluvo. "The nearest doctor's in Locust Grove. I'll drive you there."

Luluvo tried to speak, but only a muted gurgle slipped between his lips. Staring intently at Cimarron, he tried to raise a hand, but it fell back to the ground.

Cimarron reached out and gently touched the old man's shoulder as the woman kneeling next to him made a harsh sound deep in her throat, and he knew it had been a sob unsuccessfully suppressed. He rose and spoke to one of the men in the crowd. Then, with the help of the man to whom he had spoken, he lifted Luluvo, who moaned piteously, and carried him to his wagon. The old woman followed. Once Luluvo had been placed inside his wagon, Cimarron directed the woman who had been trying to care for him to stay with him. Minutes later, he was leading two horses toward Luluvo's wagon, intending to place them in the traces when a shrill scream tore through the air, freezing the gypsies in their tracks and causing the horses Cimarron was leading to bolt.

He spun around, unmindful of the fleeing horses, his hand going for his gun, and saw Rupa riding toward him, pursued by a horde of mounted men. When she screamed, he realized she had been the one who had screamed a moment ago. And then, as he left the protection of the circled wagons and went sprinting toward her, he saw for the first time the man he had sent to bring Rupa out of the woods.

His body lay slumped against Rupa's back as he sat the chestnut's rump behind the cantle of the saddle occupied by Rupa. His head lolled at an ugly angle, and as Cimarron dropped to one knee, fired, and hit the man closest to Rupa, he saw that the gypsy's head had been nearly severed from his body. An instant later, as Rupa galloped past him into the circle of wagons, he saw the bloody cavalry saber in the raised right hand of one of the riders. He knew that he was looking at the blade that had nearly decapitated the gypsy riding the chestnut behind Rupa.

Cimarron began to back away from the overwhelming tide of oncoming riders, among whom he recognized the man named Burke and his three companions whom he had seen in the restaurant in Oaks and later doing the scalp dance in Oaks' meeting hall. He leapt over a wagon tongue and then bellied down on the ground and quickly reloaded his Colt, filling all six chambers this time.

The Cherokees leveled a steady fire at the gypsies as they rode in a circle around the wagons, and the gypsies returned the fire. Cimarron's first shot brought down one of the three men who had been with Burke. As he prepared to fire a second time, a gypsy kneeling by the wagon next to him let out a groan and toppled to the ground where he lay clutching a spot just above his belt from which blood had begun to flow.

Dust rose around the wildly whooping Cherokees, blocking Cimarron's vision and delaying his shot. As he waited for the dust to clear, someone crawled under the wagon and stopped beside him. He turned his head and saw Rupa, her face streaked with dirt, a belly gun in her tense right hand.

"You all right?" he asked her, his eyes again on the Cherokee scalp hunters.

Instead of answering him, Rupa fired at a flurry of horse's legs that went rampaging past the wagon under which she and Cimarron had taken refuge.

"That gun of yours has got no range," he told her. "You—"

His words were drowned out by the fear-filled screams of women coming from behind him and blending with the desperate shouts of men.

"*Fire!*" roared a gypsy Cimarron could not see. But he could see the blazing wagon off to his left, which he realized must have been torched by one of the circling Cherokees. When he saw flaming torches appear in the hands of several other Indians, he scrambled out from under the wagon, dragging Rupa with him.

Both of them were almost bowled over as one of the camp's attackers, aboard a snorting sorrel, came careening into the center of the enclosure formed by the wagons. The man fired a series of shots, scattering the startled gypsies. Then he leapt from his horse and vanished in a cloud of dust and gunsmoke.

Another wagon's canvas cover suddenly burst into flame. From inside came a woman's tortured scream.

"Run for it," Cimarron shouted at the top of his voice to the gypsies. Then he spoke hurriedly to Rupa, giving her terse instructions. "Follow Rupa," he yelled to the gypsies.

They fled, following Rupa, who led them out of the circle of wagons as more Cherokees—some on foot, most on horseback—invaded it.

Cimarron ran to Luluvo's wagon, leapt up over the driver's seat, and bounded into its interior. He holstered his gun, picked up Luluvo, who lay huddled in one corner, an expression of absolute terror twisting his gaunt features, and then jumped to the ground from the rear of the wagon with the old man cradled in his arms. He almost fell over a wounded gypsy lying directly behind the wagon who lay writhing in pain, bullet holes in his right arm and left cheek, the top of his scalped skull a bloody expanse of red flesh and white bone.

Regaining his balance, Cimarron rounded Luluvo's wagon and ran in the direction he had told Rupa to lead the Lowara. He looked up and almost smiled when he saw that the gypsies had done what he had told Rupa to tell them to do. Nearly every tall tree surrounding the gypsy camp bore strange fruit: armed men clinging to the trees' topmost branches.

He sprinted into the forest and found the gypsy women hiding in a deep cavern beneath a slanted shelf of rimrock, Rupa among them. He deposited Luluvo on the ground, and then, after glancing at Rupa, he left the shelter. He ran to a sycamore, sprang up, caught hold of a branch, and pulled himself up into the tree. He quickly climbed it, and when he reached its top, he positioned himself on a sturdy limb and looked down at the Cherokees, all of whom were milling about in the enclosure formed by the circle of wagons, many of which were burning now.

"Pick the bastards off," Cimarron yelled to the gypsies in the trees around him.

A moment later, as a Cherokee ran out from between two wagons, Cimarron drew his gun and fired. The man went down. Wounded in the left leg, he tried to drag himself back toward the wagons, but a gypsy in a tree not far from Cimarron fired the .44–.40 in his hand and the wounded man's forehead erupted in a shower of blood and fragments of bone. He died instantly.

As the firing continued, with the gypsies pinning the Cherokees down inside the circle of burning wagons, Cimarron's attention was drawn to a cloud of dust rising in the north. He peered at it through narrowed eyes, but it was not until some minutes had passed that he was able to see several riders heading toward the Lowara camp. A few more minutes passed, and then he recognized the man riding in front of the men fanned out behind him—Kore!

They're after my ass, he thought. There's not a damned doubt about that! And me and my gypsy friends here are about to be outnumbered by more enemies than we can count. He shouted to the Lowara positioned in the trees all about him to warn them of the approach of Kore and the men riding with him.

"It's me the Tshurara want," he yelled. "I'll draw their fire away from you men while you keep those Cherokees pinned down!" He holstered his gun and quickly climbed down from his lofty perch. His boots hit the ground just as Kore and his men arrived at the camp's distant perimeter, out of sight of Burke's men, and drew rein, obviously puzzled by the sight of the ongoing gun battle, the treed gypsies, and the Cherokees pinned down within the circle of burning wagons.

Cimarron was about to head toward the Tshurara when an idea struck him. He hesitated only a moment as he considered it, and then turned and sprinted toward the blazing wagons. He leapt between two of them and landed only yards away from the man he wanted to talk to— Burke, the scalp hunter, whom he had seen in the Oaks restaurant and later as a participant in the Cherokee scalp dance. He raised his hands above his head and moved quickly in Burke's direction. No one challenged him. He doubted if any of the Cherokees had really noticed him, so busily engaged were they in battling the gypsies, who were still firing down on them from the relative safety of the trees.

"Burke," he said when he reached the man, "you're fighting the wrong people."

"We're not," Burke bellowed. "They're gypsies, aren't they?" He scowled. "What the hell are you doing here?" he asked as he apparently recognized Cimarron.

Cimarron ignored the question. "They're gypsies, all right, only they're not the gypsies you've got a quarrel with. The ones you do have a quarrel with are over there, Burke." He pointed to the spot where Kore and his men were milling about on their horses, which were shying in the face of the flames shooting skyward from the wagons.

Burke turned. "What . . ."

"Look real close, Burke. Don't you recognize any of those gypsies? They're the ones that robbed the banks and people in Oaks and Salina, not those other gypsies up there in the trees."

"By Christ on the cross, you're right!" Burke exclaimed, his eyes darting from the mounted Tshurara to the treed Lowara and back again. "I don't recollect ever seeing any of those gypsies that have treed themselves like possums before. But I sure as hell have seen most of those other ones over there walking the streets of Oaks and acting as innocent as newborn pups!"

"I'll order those gypsies in the trees to stop firing," Cimarron volunteered. "That way you and your boys'll have a chance to go after your real enemies over there. How's that sound to you, Burke? Is it a deal?"

"It's a deal!"

Cimarron, cupping his hands around his mouth, yelled to the Lowara, "*Hold your fire!*"

A moment later, Burke spoke hurriedly to the men with him and then, beckoning to them, leapt aboard his horse and galloped between two wagons, his men mounted and riding right behind him as they all headed toward Kore and the other Tshurara gypsies.

Cimarron, watching them go, smiled faintly at the expressions of surprise on the faces of the Tshurara. As Burke and the other scalp hunters bore down on them, their surprise turned quickly to alarm and then to naked fright. His smile broadened when the scalp hunters opened fire and Kore turned his horse and fled the scene with his men, the Cherokees riding hard not far behind them, both sides exchanging deadly fire.

When all of them had disappeared from sight, Cimarron left the circle formed by the wagons, some of which were now collapsing into smoldering, smoky ruins. He beckoned to the Lowara, who began to climb down from their leafy perches. As they did so, he made his way back to the cavern where he had left Luluvo. Even before he arrived at the spot, he heard loud wailing, which grew louder still the nearer he came to his destination.

When he caught his first glimpse of the women who had earlier taken refuge at the spot, he was startled to find them huddled on the ground, their hair unbound, their clothes ripped, and their arms wrapped around their bent bodies as they wept and wailed.

He went up to Rupa, who stood silently, her face solemn, some distance away from the other women. "What's

170

wrong?" he asked her, suspecting that he knew the answer to his question.

"Luluvo is dying," she answered, and he saw two tears ease from the corners of her eyes and slide down her cheeks.

"The fighting back there's all over, so now I can drive Luluvo in to the doctor in Locust Grove."

As Cimarron started to move away from Rupa, she reached out and seized his arm. "There is nothing a doctor can do for him now."

Cimarron, unconvinced and unwilling to give up hope for the old man, made his way to Luluvo. When he reached him, he noted two things: the paleness of the man's skin, and the fact that blood still flowed from his throat wound, indicating that his heart still pumped. He hunkered down beside the badly wounded man and placed two fingers against his throat. The pulse he felt there was weak.

"Luluvo," he said softly, "can you hear me?"

Luluvo's eyelids, which had been closed, flickered and then opened. He blinked. Smiled faintly. "Cimarron." The name had been spoken softly, barely audibly.

"I'm going to drive you in to the doctor, Luluvo."

The old man's head moved slightly, a negative gesture. "I go to God, Cimarron. Don't delay me." He managed to raise his hand from the ground. As it started to fall back, Cimarron reached out and gripped it.

"The Indians . . ."

"The fight's over," Cimarron said when Luluvo's voice faded away into silence.

"You helped again."

"Listen, Luluvo, the doctor—"

"No."

Cimarron felt Luluvo's weak hold on his hand momentarily strengthen and then relax.

"It is good the way I die," Luluvo murmured.

No way's a good way to die, Cimarron thought, and the anger he felt surging within him surprised him.

"We gypsies die outdoors. We may not be born nor may we die inside. Death, like birth, pollutes."

Behind Cimarron and Luluvo, an old woman began to chant in the Romany language, a sad and melancholy melody that threaded through the sound of the other women's weeping.

"Rupa," Luluvo whispered weakly.

Cimarron went and got her. When he was once again hunkered down beside Luluvo with Rupa kneeling beside him, the old man turned his gaze on Rupa and said, "Do not throw the gold coins you would ordinarily toss into my grave."

Rupa started to protest, but the look in Luluvo's eyes silenced her.

"Tell the Lowara," he said, "to give Cimarron the eighty-seven dollars he told me Mala of the Tshurara had swindled from his friend, Miss Serena Farthing, in Muskogee."

"You will need that money in the Nation of the Dead," Rupa protested, her voice unsteady, her eyes wet.

"Do as I say, woman," Luluvo ordered in a suddenly firm voice. "Say that you will!"

"I will," Rupa said, and sobbed.

As Cimarron put an arm around her, Luluvo murmured, "Be my witness, Cimarron."

He waited while Luluvo painfully caught his breath.

"Tell the Lowara that Rupa is the one who must take my place as their leader."

Rupa's eyes widened in surprise. She glanced at Cimarron, who said, "I think you've made a real good choice, Luluvo."

"Rupa is brave. She rescued you from the river and from the Tshurara. She is bold. She made Kore unclean by displaying herself so impudently to him. She will make a good leader of my people."

Cimarron nodded and tightened his hold on Rupa, who was openly weeping now, her head lowered, her arms hanging limply at her sides.

"I bid you both good-bye," Luluvo whispered. "Go away from me now. Leave me alone."

When neither Cimarron nor Rupa moved, Luluvo lifted his head slightly, pointed a trembling finger at them, and ordered, "Go!"

They left him.

When they were some distance away from the cavern, the wailing of the women a mournful sea of sound behind them, Cimarron asked, "Why didn't Luluvo want us to stay with him anymore?"

"It is a gypsy custom," Rupa replied. "When one is dying, he must seek to sever his bonds with the living."

They stood there then, Cimarron with his arm still around Rupa's waist, in a somber silence that was broken some time later by a sudden and skull-shattering shriek. They both turned in time to see a woman, perhaps the one who had just cried out so disconsolately, throw herself on Luluvo.

They looked at each other, neither of them speaking, and then they walked back together through the crowd of women to find what Cimarron was sure they would find.

Luluvo was dead and even the ample body of the grief-stricken woman lying across him could not warm his body, which was already beginning to turn cold.

Three days later, on a morning made brilliant by bright sunshine, Cimarron stood among the gypsies and watched two men use ropes to lower Luluvo's pine coffin into an open grave. He listened to the music made by one of the Lowara men on a partially charred violin he had salvaged from the wreckage of his wagon. He continued watching the unfolding ceremony: one of the men stepped up to the open grave, opened a bottle of rum, poured some of it on the coffin, tasted the bottle's contents, and then handed it to a man in the crowd. When the bottle reached him as it passed from hand to hand, Cimarron drank from it and then gave it to the next man.

"*Akana mukava tut le Devlesa*," he said softly, addressing the dead Luluvo and using the words Rupa had taught him earlier: "I now leave you to God."

173

Later, when the grave had been filled, he joined the gypsies in what Rupa had told him was the *pomana*, or funeral, meal. Before sitting down to it, he, like each of the gypsies, said aloud, "*Te avel angla tue, Luluvo, kodo khabe tai kado pimo tai meange pe sastimaste*," a salutation Rupa had also taught him earlier. She had explained to him that it was used before and after the *pomana*, and she translated the words for him: "May this food be before you, Luluvo, and in your memory, and may it profit us in good health and in good spirit."

Later, when the *pomana* ended and the gypsies began to disperse, Cimarron sought out Rupa, and when he found her standing and sadly surveying the wreckage of the Lowara's wagons, he put his arm around her and said, "I've got to be on my way."

She turned to gaze at him, saying nothing. And then, dipping a hand into one of the pockets in her skirt, she drew money from it. "Eighty-seven dollars," she said. "What Mala did was wrong. She should not have swindled your friend, Miss Farthing. Gypsies like Mala give all gypsies a bad name."

"Honey, I can't take this money from you. You folks are going to need it to buy new wagons, food, clothes—all sorts of things to help you get back on your feet."

Rupa reached out and closed his fingers around the money. "Before you go . . ." Her words trailed away.

"What have you got in mind, honey?"

She sighed. "Cimarron, you have made a mark on me, one that is invisible but there nonetheless. I want to make my mark on you."

He leaned over and kissed her. "You have, honey. You truly have. It's been just fine knowing you, and I'm not likely ever to forget you."

Rupa told him then what she had in mind, surprising him at first. But then he grinned and said, "Sure, if that's what you want to do."

She led him to her wagon, which, miraculously, had been only slightly damaged during the fiery battle with

174

the Cherokee scalp hunters, and busied herself inside it for several minutes while he waited on a stool nearby. When she was ready, she turned to him, a sharp needle in one hand, a bowl containing a liquid she had prepared in the other.

Working swiftly and expertly with the needle, she tattooed a tiny, almost imperceptible diamond between Cimarron's right eye and the bridge of his nose, puncturing his skin till the blood spurted, then dipping her needle in the liquid she had prepared, and then repeating the entire process.

When she was finished, she held up a mirror and he stared into it.

"I once met a sailor on the Barbary Coast," he remarked, grinning, "who had a naked lady tattooed on his back. But this sure is a different kind of tattooing. This is how the gypsies do it?"

"We would never use erotic designs. Nor would we tattoo the body. Only the face—the eyes, the cheeks, the chin, or the forehead. Now, if you should meet other gypsies, they will see the mark I have made upon you and they will know without you having to tell them that you are one of the Rom.

"There is something else. Do not wash the tattoo for three days. When it heals, you will have a blue mark there that most people will not even notice, but we believe such a tattoo will drive away all evil spells and maladies."

"I'm obliged to you, Rupa." Cimarron rose.

She rose with him, then, using a linen kerchief, she blotted the blood she had drawn from him.

"If I were free," she murmured, her cheek pressing against his chest, "if I did not have to lead my people as Luluvo wanted me to do, we could—" She looked up at him. "But you cannot stay with me. And now I cannot go with you."

He nodded.

"Perhaps it is just as well." She smiled faintly. "I think in time you would make me an unhappy woman. A shrew, perhaps."

175

"Now, what makes you say a think like that to me, honey?"

Rupa's smile broadened. "You could never be happy with just one woman, Cimarron. I know the kind of man you are. Where women are concerned, you—" She paused. Then, wagging a playful finger at him, she said, "We Rom have a saying. *Kay jala i suv shay jala wi o thav.*'"

"What might that mean?"

" 'Where the needle goes, surely the thread will follow.' That, it seems to me, sums up you and your attraction to women, Cimarron. You just can't help yourself."

He gave her a rueful smile.

She gave him a kiss.

That afternoon, as Cimarron rode away from the camp of his blood brothers, the Lowara gypsies, with Varnum handcuffed and riding beside him, he was whistling as he fondly remembered Rupa and found himself hoping that someday, somewhere he would meet her again so that they could . . .

His whistling grew louder and more lilting as his arousing thoughts raged.

They had not gone far from the camp when Varnum suddenly gave a startled grunt.

Cimarron, who had been drifting in an erotic reverie involving Rupa, snapped alert. His eyes narrowed as he saw what it was that had caused Varnum's reaction.

Corpses.

The corpses of Kore and the men who had been riding with him. They were all sprawled haphazardly on the ground in a sun-dappled glade. All of them had been scalped.

Cimarron stared down at the crusted blood covering the spots where their hair had been—the blood on which black ants and buzzing flies were feeding.

He stared, his expression grim, at the numerous stab wounds and bullet holes in the bodies.

Those Cherokee scalp hunters, he thought as he rode on with his prisoner, they sure did get what they went after.

He didn't look back.

1

Cimarron halted his bay in the shade of a blackjack oak and
mopped his neck and face with his blue bandanna. There were
dark-brown circles underneath his arms, in sharp contrast to
the light brown of the rest of his shirt. He was thinking about
the soothing bromide baths the hotel in Sulphur Springs offered, and hoped that he'd have time for one. At the very least,
it would do his shoulder wound some good. He had come close
to catching up to Billy White-Face in Chickasaw Nation, but
he'd caught a bullet in the shoulder, instead. His wound was
just a crease, but it had bled worse than it should have, and the
constant perspiring had set it to stinging something fierce. He
owed White-Face a thorny debt.

"Soon, Billy White-Face," Cimarron muttered to himself, "real
soon."

He took a short drink from his canteen and then replaced
it on his saddle horn. As he rode on, he was careful not to

push the bay because the horse was even more tired than he was.

Cimarron had been chasing his quarry through the Nations for two weeks now and the more fatigued and sore he got, the more determined he became that he was going to bring the Comanchero leader back to Fort Smith with him—to hang.

The deputy marshal knew he had no business condemning the man—or sentencing him—before Judge Parker could, but somehow Cimarron felt that rape and mass murder were definitely hanging offenses.

Cimarron had dealt with Comancheros before, but that was in Texas and New Mexico, before he'd pinned on a lawman's star. In fact, in those days he'd even run with a couple of bands, but never men like Billy White-Face. Even during his days of following the owlhoot trail, Cimarron had never been an animal—and that's all Billy White-Face was.

The Comanchero had come up with his band from Texas. Apparently, White-Face had heard that the Nations were easy pickings. In spite of the fact that the Comancheros had wreaked their own special brand of havoc on the Nations for weeks, Cimarron was determined to prove the man wrong. When Marshal Upham had first sent him out from Fort Smith to track down Billy White-Face and his band of cutthroat half-breeds, Mexicans, Indians, and deserters, it had just been another job, but every time another muscle ached, it became more and more personal.

The trail had finally led here, to Choctaw Nation, and there was every indication that White-Face was heading for Sulphur Springs—or, at least, in that direction—alone. White-Face had split his men up, probably planning to meet with them later. What Cimarron had to do was catch up with him before that happened because it would be a lot easier to take the man if he didn't have his band of killers to back him up.

Cimarron was a rangy, rawboned man who, even when he was exhausted, managed to ride tall in the saddle, appearing relaxed. His shoulders were broad and his arms heavily muscled. His stirrups had been hung low to comfortably accommodate his long, lean legs.

He was constantly alert and knew that many of the men that he had tracked—including Billy White-Face—were also wary.

The slightest outward sign of fatigue could be construed as weakness, and showing weakness to a desperado would be like showing a red flag to a bull.

Perspiration continued to soak the taut skin of his sun-bronzed face. His face had a weathered and rugged look, made menacing by the firm set of his thin lips, the sharp slant of his nose, and his prominent cheekbones set over slightly sunken cheeks. A scar—a shiny gray line of dead flesh—ran from just below his left eye, over his cheek, and ended at the corner of his mouth.

He had ridden on for another half-hour when his keen senses alerted him to the sound of approaching horses—four or five, from the sound of them and the amount of dust they were kicking up. He reined in and waited, his entire body poised to react.

When the riders finally came into full view, he breathed a small sigh of relief but remained on the alert. From all appearances, the approaching riders were Choctaw Lighthorsemen, members of the Indian police patrol that kept the law in the Choctaw Nation.

"Howdy," Cimarron greeted them as they reined in before him. He figured they were simply on a routine ride and not hunting someone down because their horses did not look as if they had been pushed.

The man in the lead nodded slightly and Cimarron went on. "I'm looking for a lone rider, a white man you'd remember seeing. He's got a white beard and mustache and bushy white eyebrows," he said, listing the trademarks of Billy White-Face.

"You hunt this man?" the leader asked.

"That's right."

"Why?"

"I'm a deputy marshal out of Fort Smith. This man has committed crimes for which he must pay. I'm here to see that he does."

The man stared silently at Cimarron until the deputy reached into the pocket of his faded jeans and produced his badge.

"We have seen no such man."

Frowning, Cimarron returned the star to his pocket, then brightened.

"He's riding a dappled gray with a white tail." They'd sure as hell remember if they saw that.

The leader turned and spoke to the man on his right, then did the same with the man on his left. When he looked at Cimarron again, his expression—what there was of it—had not changed.

"We have seen such a horse," he said.

"Where?"

"Between here and the Kiamichi River, at a small wooden house. The horse was tied outside."

"Still saddled?"

The Choctaw nodded.

White-Face was visiting someone, Cimarron thought, or else why not unsaddle the horse? Visiting . . . or victimizing?

"When was this?"

"Yesterday."

"Do you know who the house belongs to?"

"It has belonged to many people," the Choctaw said with a shrug. "It will belong to many more."

"How do I get there?"

The man turned slightly in his saddle and pointed north, saying, "Make for the river in a straight line and you will come to it."

"I am grateful."

The Lighthorseman nodded, and then they all continued on their way. Cimarron watched them until they were out of sight, and then headed for the Kiamichi River. He hoped that White-Face had no intention of hooking up with Hell's Highway. Cimarron had already traveled that path more than he liked.

When Cimarron came to a house that was virtually in the middle of nowhere, he halted his bay and examined it. This must have been the house the Lighthorseman had told him about, but at the moment there was no horse tied up in front of it. Smoke, however, escaped from the chimney, evidence that someone was living there.

He decided to approach the house on foot, stealthily, in case White-Face was inside. Tying his horse to a tree trunk, he drew his gun and began his approach. He reached the front porch without incident, but instead of mounting it, he moved around to check the back. He spotted a lean-to with some hay in it, but it was otherwise empty. He went back to the left side of the house and peered in a window.

He saw a woman tending to a pot on a stove, and for a moment he forgot White-Face and, with the pure enjoyment of a man who dearly loved women, watched her as she moved around the room. She had wheat-colored hair pinned atop her head, revealing a long, graceful neck. Full-breasted and full-hipped, she moved with a kind of grace that made it seem as if she was gliding across the floor instead of walking.

What possible business could she have had with someone like Billy White-Face?

Well, the only way to answer that was to ask her.

Satisfied that she was alone in the house, he moved back to the front, mounted the porch, and knocked on the door. He just had time to holster his gun before she answered it.

Up close he saw that she had clear blue eyes, a strong nose, and a wide, full-lipped mouth. She was a real beauty, this one.

"Can I help you?" she asked in a voice that tickled his spine.

"Yes, ma'am," he said. "I was wondering if you could spare something to eat? Or something cold to drink? I've been riding for a long time and I seem to have run out of supplies."

She gave him a frank up-and-down look of appraisal—like he was a horse she was thinking of bidding on—and then looked past him and asked, "Where's your horse?"

"I tied him to a tree a little ways back. I didn't want to scare you by riding up bold as day, seeing as how you're a woman alone and all."

She grinned and asked, "How did you know I was a woman alone?"

"I didn't see any indications that there was a man around."

"Well," she said, giving him a bold look this time, "there sure is now. Why don't you bring your horse closer and then come on in. I'll have something waiting for you."

Cimarron had an idea of what he hoped she'd have waiting for him, but he said, "That's right nice of you, ma'am. I appreciate it."

"I don't have a barn, but there's a lean-to in the back with some hay where you can put your horse."

"That'll be fine."

"By the way," she said, "what's your name?"

"Cimarron, ma'am."

"My name is Cora Carson, Cimarron. When you get back, come right in. I won't lock the door," she said, and then closed it gently behind her.

Cimarron was conscious of the swelling bulge in his jeans as he walked back to retrieve his horse, a swelling he was sure Cora Carson would have put there even if he hadn't gone without a woman for over a week now. For a man who appreciated women like Cimarron did, going that long without one was an uncommon occurrence indeed.

Hopefully, his personal drought was over.

After Cimarron had cared for his horse, he entered through the unlocked door and found Cora Carson standing at the table.

"Do you like jackrabbit stew?" she asked.

"Very much."

"Sit down, then," she said. "Eat."

"Are you eating, too?"

"Oh, yes."

He sat and she sat across from him. He shifted in his chair, trying to find a comfortable position where the pressure would not be so great on his swelling manhood.

"You live here alone?" he asked.

"Most of the time," she answered, and then said, "Occasionally I have . . . visitors."

Men visitors, he thought, and he couldn't blame them. The fact that she admitted that made him even more hopeful of ending his unscheduled period of celibacy—while not losing sight of his primary goal, of course.

"Do you give them all jackrabbit stew?"

"I give them whatever I have on hand."

"Aren't you afraid to be living out here alone?"

"I prefer it."

"The Nations is no place for a woman alone, Cora," he said.

"The Choctaw don't bother me, Cimarron," she answered. And then, smiling broadly, she said, "We trade with each other."

He didn't wonder what it was she traded with.

After dinner she cleaned the table, and then, as she brought him coffee, he asked, "I wonder if you haven't seen a friend of mine who was supposed to be passing this way."

"What's his name?"

"Billy," Cimarron said. "He has a white beard—"

"Cimarron," she said, interrupting him.

"Yeah?"

"You been looking at me since you been here, am I right?" she asked, meeting his eyes coyly.

"Of course you're right, Cora," Cimarron said. "It'd be right hard for any man not to look at a lovely woman like yourself, especially someone like me who appreciates lovely women and has been on the trail for so long."

"Ah," she said, nodding and smiling, "you've had a lot of women, have you?"

"Some," he said, shrugging. "I'm not a bragging man by nature, but I've had my share of women."

"You must really know how to pleasure a woman then, huh?" she asked.

He smiled and said, "I know a way or two."

Her grin widened into a smile now and suddenly she slid into his lap, her weight warm and firm. She wiggled her buttocks against his erection and said, "My Lord, you're a big one, aren't you?"

"Big enough."

He put his arms around her and drew her mouth to his. There was nothing tentative about her kiss. Her tongue moved slowly over his teeth, and then pushed past them into his mouth. She moaned as he pushed it back into her mouth with his own.

Abruptly she leapt off his lap and her hands worked feverishly at the buttons on the front of her dress. She stepped out of it, revealing her large, full breasts, with their pink, already erect nipples.

"Cimarron," she sighed, moving close to him so that he could bury his face in the valley between her breasts, then capture one nipple in his mouth.

"Oh, Cimarron," she moaned, clutching at his head, "the bed, quickly. I want to see you naked. I want to feel you inside of me . . ."

He stood up, lifted her effortlessly off the floor, and carried her to the pallet against the far wall. He placed her gently on the bed and then started to undress. As he did so, she slid her dress farther down, over her hips, until it was gathered around her ankles. She kicked it away and reclined fully on the bed, eager for him to join her.

"Oh!" she gasped as he slid his jeans down over his hips and his erection sprang free, standing straight out. "It's the biggest I've ever seen!"

"I make do with it," he said, removing his boots and pants. When he removed his shirt, she marveled at his broad shoulders and muscular arms, but her attention kept going back to the huge member between his legs.

"Bring it closer," she said.

He obliged and she took him in her hands reverently, sliding her right hand up and down his erection while cupping his balls with her left. When she leaned forward to take him into her mouth, Cimarron moaned and leaned into her. Then she threw herself down on the pallet, pulling him down on top of her.

He knelt on the thin pallet between her legs and licked her nipples before he prodded her damp portal with the head of his shaft.

"Yes," she whispered, locking her legs around his hips and pressing her heels against his buttocks.

He moaned as he slid into her, feeling as if he were coming home after being away a long while. But just as he let out a sigh of relief, the door was kicked open and a man leapt into the room.

"What—" Cimarron cried, looking over his shoulder. If the man had a gun, Cimarron would have been dead, but instead the intruder lunged with a knife clutched in his right hand, held low, the way an experienced knife-fighter would hold it.

Cimarron tried to withdraw from Cora, but the woman's legs were locked around him and she did not seem anxious to release him.

"Let me go, woman," he shouted as the man started across the floor toward them.

"No, no," she moaned, reaching for him with her hands as well.

"Cora, dammit—" he started to shout, but then he realized she was not holding on to him out of passion. She was trying to make it easy for the knife-fighter to kill him.

"Sorry, Cora," he muttered, and struck her on the jaw with his right fist. Her face went slack and, finally, her legs went limp and he was free.

The other man was on him by then, and as Cimarron turned, the knife was thrust toward him. He moved to his right in an attempt to avoid it, and only partially succeeded in doing so. The knife slashed him on his right side, but he had no time to pay attention to the pain.

The knife thrust had, for all intents and purposes, missed him, and the blow threw the man off balance. Cimarron hit him with a short right in the face, and the man staggered backward, retaining his hold on the knife.

Cimarron looked down at the floor where his gunbelt lay underneath his pants, but decided against going after it. Instead, he steeled himself for the man's next attack. He felt more naked at that moment than he had ever felt in his life.

The man came in slowly now, holding the knife steady, grinning at Cimarron.

"I'm gonna cut off that big meat of yours, lawman," he said, "and stuff it in your mouth."

Cimarron did not reply, but the significance of the man's remark did not elude him. Both he and the woman must have already known Cimarron was a lawman, and they'd been waiting to catch him in this trap—a trap very probably set by Billy White-Face.

Cimarron was aware of the blood oozing down his side, and now the old bullet wound was aching again, but he kept his eyes on the man. As the knife-fighter came closer, the lawman suddenly kicked out with his bare right foot, lifting his pants off the floor, tossing them at his opponent. The pants landed on the knife, giving Cimarron time to move for his gun. As his hand closed over it, the man tossed the pants across the room, freeing the knife. Cimarron unleathered the gun, cocked it, and fired as the man lunged at him again.

The bullet caught his attacker in the throat and he staggered back, gagging on his own blood. He dropped the knife and wrapped both hands around the wound, attempting to stem the flow of blood, but it did no good. His eyes glazed over and he fell to the floor, dead.

At that same moment Cora moaned on the bed, slowly coming awake. Cimarron turned, moved to the bed, and leaned over her so that he would be the first thing she saw when she woke up.

"Cimarron?" she said, frowning.

"Hello, Cora."

She stared at him a moment, smiled as if she were still putting on her act, then suddenly frowned as she remembered what had happened.

"Ben," she said quickly, trying to rise, "where's Ben?"

"Is that the fella with the knife?"

"Yeah."

"Is he your man?"

"Yeah."

"Well, you're going to have to find another man, Cora."

"You killed him?" she screamed, trying to rise again.

He put his free hand in the center of her firm breasts and pushed her back down. "Where's White-Face, Cora?"

"What?"

"White-Face," he said again. "Billy White-Face. He put you up to this. Where is he?"

She stared at him for a moment, fear in her eyes—fear of him, or of White-Face, he wondered—and then said, "I can't tell you."

"Yes you can."

"No, he'll kill me."

"Cora," Cimarron said, smiling, "you and me were really getting into it before your friend broke in, right?"

"Right," she said. Then she put on a smile and said in a seductive voice, "That's right, Cimarron, we were. Do you want to get back to it? I'm still ready."

There had been no mistaking the fact that she had been ready before. Cimarron knew when a woman was truly ready. Apparently Cora enjoyed her work.

"Cimarron?" she asked, assuming a seductive look. His hand was still between her breasts and she took it now and placed it directly over one of them, rubbing her nipple with his hand. He felt her harden.

187

She thrust her hips up at him and he could smell her, feeling his flesh involuntarily harden again. But as she closed her eyes, Cimarron placed the barrel of the gun firmly under her chin, then cocked the hammer back for effect.

"Y-you wouldn't!" she stammered.

"Yes, I would, Cora. I may have done some trifling in my time, but I'm not a man to be trifled with." His green eyes bore coldly into her surprised blue ones, and she knew that he was telling the truth.

"Now, you'll tell me where Billy White-Face is, won't you?"

Cora told Cimarron that her man, Ben, used to ride with Billy White-Face and that Ben thought they were still friends—or at least, that's what he told her. The truth of the matter was that Ben was afraid of White-Face, to the point where he would even let White-Face have at Cora whenever he passed through. That's what had happened the day before Cimarron's arrival. White-Face had shown up, eaten, had his way with Cora, and then told both of them that a lawman might pass by, and if he did, they were to follow his instructions.

"So, simple as that, you agreed to murder a man," Cimarron said, "a lawman, to boot."

"He would have killed us."

"Well, your man got killed anyway, didn't he?" Cimarron reminded her.

"He wasn't much of a man anyway. Will you take the gun away? It's cold."

"Are you going to tell me where White-Face went?"

"He said he was heading for Sulphur Springs. He was talking about getting one of those special baths, you know—what do you call them?"

"Bromide."

"Yeah, that's it."

"In Sulphur Springs?"

"That's what he said, honest."

Cimarron decided to believe her, and withdrew his gun.

"Then that's where I'm going," he said.

While she watched, he dressed, being careful of both his wounds. The bullet crease was all but healed, though still sore, and the knife cut had already stopped bleeding.

"Billy's fast with a gun, you know," she told him. "You probably wouldn't be able to match him if you were healthy, let alone hurt like you are. Why don't you stay here with me, Cimarron?"

"I've got a job to do."

"I think you're going to end up dead doing it," Cora said, sounding sad. "Billy White-Face is one of the fastest guns around."

"Then I'll just have to hope I'm smarter than him," Cimarron said, putting on his hat. As he went out the door, he added to himself, "Hope and pray."

About the Author

LEO P. KELLEY was born and raised in Pennsylvania's Wyoming Valley and spent a good part of his boyhood exploring the surrounding mountains, hunting and fishing. He served in the Army Security Agency as a cryptographer, and then went "on the road," working as dishwasher, laborer, etc. He later joined the Merchant Marine and sailed on tankers calling at Texan, South American, and Italian ports. In New York City he attended the New School for Social Research, receiving a BA in Literature. He worked in advertising, promotion, and marketing before leaving the business world to write full time.

Mr. Kelley has published a dozen novels and has several others now in the works. He has also published many short stories in leading magazines.

JOIN THE *CIMMARON* READERS' PANEL

Help us bring you more of the books you like by filling out this survey and mailing it in today.

1. Book Title: _____

   Book #: _____

2. Using the scale below, how would you rate this book on the following features? Please write in one rating from 0-10 for each feature in the spaces provided.

POOR		NOT SO GOOD			O.K.			GOOD		EXCEL-LENT
0	1	2	3	4	5	6	7	8	9	10

                                                              RATING
Overall opinion of book .... _____
Plot/Story .... _____
Setting/Location .... _____
Writing Style .... _____
Character Development .... _____
Conclusion/Ending .... _____
Scene on Front Cover .... _____

3. About how many western books do you buy for yourself each month? _____

4. How would you classify yourself as a reader of westerns?
   I am a ( ) light ( ) medium ( ) heavy reader.

5. What is your education?
   ( ) High School (or less) ( ) 4 yrs. college
   ( ) 2 yrs. college   ( ) Post Graduate

6. Age _____   7. Sex: ( ) Male ( ) Female

Please Print Name_____

Address_____

City _____ State _____ Zip _____

Phone # ( )_____

Thank you. Please send to New American Library, Research Dept., 1633 Broadway, New York, NY 10019.

Exciting Westerns by Jon Sharpe

Prices higher in Canada
